POSSESSED

A SCI-FI ALIEN WARRIOR ROMANCE

RAIDER WARLORDS OF THE VANDAR
BOOK ONE

TANA STONE

BROADMOOR BOOKS

I sacrificed myself to save my sister's ship. Now the raider warlord owns me.

It was my own fault. I was the navigator of our ship, and I'm the one who led us straight into Vandar territory. We'd heard rumors about the Vandar raiders—everyone in the galaxy had. Terrifying and ruthless, they were a scourge on the Zagrath empire and destroyed everything in their path. Few had actually laid eyes on the Vandar or the notorious warlords who led their fleets of warships—and survived to talk about it.

So, when the ruthless aliens boarded our ship intent on destroying it and killing the crew, I did the only thing I could do. I gave myself to the dark and menacing warlord.

In exchange for allowing my sister's ship passage out of the Vandar territory, I must share his bed and travel with his crew of deadly raiders. Even though the sight of the huge, battle-scarred alien terrifies me.

But as I adjust to my new life on a savage warship, I discover that the dominant alien warrior wants more than just my body. He wants to possess my soul. And he'll make a new deal with me to get it.

CHAPTER
ONE

Astrid

It was all my fault.

There was no one who would argue with that—not even my sister—and she loved to argue with me about almost anything.

Of course, it had been an accident. I hadn't intended to let our ship drift into Vandar territory. No one in their right mind would purposely enter Vandar space. Not when the raiders patrolled so intently, seeking the slightest excuse to go after a ship and strip it for everything—supplies, weapons, crew.

"How far are we from the neutral zone?" my sister screamed over the sirens wailing on the bridge.

I stared down at my fingers on the console, frozen above the blinking lights indicating our position. Even though I

1

was looking at the coordinates, I couldn't focus on what they meant. The warning lights that made the skin on my hands glow red had caused my brain to short-circuit.

"Astrid!"

Her sharp voice jolted me out of my daze, and I spun around at the navigational controls to face my sister. Her hands gripped the armrests of the captain's chair, her knuckles white. "What?"

With her red hair pulled up into a wild bun on top of her head and mine ash blonde and painfully straight, we looked as about different as sisters could. And while she was tall and lean, I was most definitely not. The only thing we shared were sea-green eyes, and right now, hers were flashing with fury. "How much longer do we have to outfly these asshole raiders?"

"Right." I pivoted back around and took a deep breath, trying to steady my racing heart and the thoughts ping-ponging through my brain. Did our old freighter stand a chance against a Vandar warbird? What would happen if they caught us? Were the rumors true?

I gave a hard shake of my head. Now was not the time to let my mind go down a rabbit hole.

Focus, Astrid. You can do this.

Even though I couldn't even hear it over the sirens, I hummed to myself as I moved my hands across the console. The vibrations in my throat calmed me, as they always had, even if the readouts were less than comforting.

I turned back around to face my sister. "We're still .3 astronomical units away from the neutral zone."

"Fuck!" Tara jumped out of her chair and took long steps over to my station, dropping her head close to mine. "How did this happen?"

I flinched at the implied rebuke, even though it wasn't the

worst I'd gotten. The truth was, I was a crapola navigator, and everyone on board knew it. The only reason I had the job at all was because this was my big sister's ship, and she'd put me where she thought I could do the least amount of damage. So much for that.

"I don't know." I didn't meet her eyes, because I couldn't bear to see the disappointment in them. "I might have calculated wrong."

"Or you might not have been paying attention again."

I cut my eyes to the pilot at the console next to mine. Even though his eyes were locked on the front view screen, his jaw was tight, and I knew he could hear us.

"I'm really sorry, Tar—"

"Save it." She stood. "We'll talk about this later. Right now, I need you focused."

I tried to ignore the burning behind my eyes as she strode back to her chair. I could only imagine how our talk later would go. Probably a lot like the others where she lectured me on responsibility and how lucky we were.

I glanced around the dingy, gray bridge of the battered freighter. Sure, it may be a big deal for a woman to captain her own freighter—especially a woman as young as my sister —but transporting other people's junk around the galaxy in a ship that had seen better days was not my idea of a good time —or a good life. Not that I could ever say that to my sister. Or ever would.

Despite hating that she still treated me like a child and was bossy as hell, Tara was all I had. It had been just the two of us since we were teenagers, and I knew that as much as she threatened, she would never actually drop me off at an alien outpost.

"Brace," the first officer cried, seconds before the entire

ship shuddered, rocking to one side and almost sending me flying off my seat.

"Report!" Tara yelled.

"A direct hit on our starboard. Hull breach in one of our cargo bays."

I swiveled to look at Tara. Our cargo bays held all the merchandise and weapons we were transporting from one outpost of the Zagrath Empire to another.

An expression I didn't recognize flashed across her face, but then she narrowed her eyes and looked straight ahead. "If they think that's going to slow us down, they don't know us very well."

Another hit jolted me so hard my teeth rattled. I clutched the edges of the console to keep myself steady, peering down at the navigational route and the flashing, blue dot that indicated our ship moving slowly across the curved, green line toward the neutral zone where we would be safe. Of course, the reality was that the Vandar raiders didn't observe the borders of the neutral zone any more than they observed the rules of war. I knew, just like every person on board, that reaching our destination did not guarantee our safety. Nothing could do that in the face of one of the brutal warlords who led their menacing hordes of black warbirds that were said to materialize out of thin air.

More red photon fire exploded across our bow.

"Get us out of here, Mose," my sister said, over the sound of more weapons firing.

"I'm trying, Captain. But propulsion systems are failing."

Despite the sirens and the explosions, the bridge seemed to go quiet for a moment. We all turned to face Tara. Tendrils fell out of her bun and curled around her face, blending with the red splotches of color on her cheeks.

She pressed her lips together. "They'll tear us apart if we

keep going, and we're not going to be able to outrun them." Her eyes flicked to her first officer, standing slightly behind her at a console. "Power down, and tell the Vandar we surrender. Maybe they'll take our remaining cargo in exchange for our safe passage out of the sector."

Bile rose in my throat, and I put a hand over my mouth to keep it down, turning away so no one could see my weakness. Not even Tara believed what she was saying. The Vandar would never let us go. We'd all heard the stories. The Vandar were not known for their mercy, or for negotiating.

I couldn't bear to look back at my sister. She knew this as well as any of us, but her voice did not tremble with fear like mine would have. She would be brave to the end.

My stomach churned. My sister was going to lose everything, and all because I'd been too distracted to do my job.

Our ship slowed, and the engines ceased rumbling. Soon after, the weapons fire also stopped, and several black-hulled ships appeared off our front bow, almost melting into the darkness of space behind them.

My pulse skittered, and I heard the sharp inhalation of breath around me. The enemy ships looked like massive birds in mid-flight, with arched wings stretching out iron claws from a round belly. I almost expected them to have red eyes that glowed.

Another hard jolt told me the Vandar raiders had locked onto our ship.

"They're boarding us," Mose said, his voice toneless.

I finally turned to look at my sister. I needed to talk to her before they came. I needed to tell her how sorry I was.

She hadn't moved, her arms straight and rigid and her hands curled around the armrests of her chair. Her chin jutted up and her shoulders were squared. She knew the evil that approached, and she planned to meet it with the same steely determination she'd always had, and I'd always admired.

I attempted to catch her eyes, but her gaze was fixed over me. As the pounding of boots on the metal floor grew louder, she tilted her head up almost imperceptibly. "Let them come."

CHAPTER

TWO

Kratos

"It's some sort of freighter." My battle chief leaned against the dark standing console, as he glanced down at the readouts.

I rocked back on the heels of my boots, peering out the front of my warbird at the outmatched space vessel we were pursuing. "I can see that. Is it Zagrath?"

"It's not an empire ship, but it looks like it has Zagrath access identifiers," Corvak said after stealing another look at his blinking screen.

"*Tvek*," I cursed, a low growl escaping my lips. "That means it's carrying cargo for the empire. Could be guns or supplies to keep our enemy well-stocked to ravage more planets like ours."

Other dark rumbles of anger from my command deck

warriors joined mine. I didn't need to look at my crew to know the fury on my warriors' faces.

My gaze locked on the battered ship we were chasing. It didn't look like much, but that didn't mean it wasn't dangerous. Any ship moving supplies around the massive, Zagrath Empire was a threat to the freedom of those not wishing to live under choking imperial rule. I clenched a fist tightly as I thought about the greedy empire that had taken over our planet generations ago and forced our nomadic warrior people to take to space.

"How long until we're within firing range?" I asked, assessing quickly that the freighter was no match for our advanced weaponry.

I knew that my horde was massed behind us, flying in the amoeba attack formation that we preferred, the sleek ships shifting positions intermittently. We'd dropped our invisibility shielding when we'd determined that the ship we were pursuing was no threat, so it was standard procedure to fly in amoeba to make us harder to target.

"Closing in now. Should I prepare a torpedo, Raas Kratos?" My battle chief addressed me by my full Vandar title, as he always did when confirming an attack.

I glanced at the warrior who was also my cousin, his black hair tied back. Corvak was so eager to fire, but I preferred to mete out our violence in controlled doses.

I strode a few steps closer to the view screen that stretched across the front of the command deck, my leather kilt slapping my bare thighs. Something about the ship piqued my attention, and I wanted to know why it had flown into our territory when most ships went out of their way to avoid us. Were they exceptionally daring or exceptionally stupid?

"No." I crossed my arms, the crossbody strap that kept my

steel shoulder armor in place digging into my flesh. "They might have valuable cargo. We'll board them."

Another rumble passed through my command deck crew like a wave—one of anticipation. We hadn't boarded a ship in a while, and the possibility of battle fired their lust for enemy blood. I know it fired mine.

I turned and took long steps back across the command deck, nodding at my first officer and Corvak as I passed them. "You're with me."

They both grunted in acknowledgement, spinning on their heels to join me, the leather of their kilts catching air and their long tails swishing. Like all Vandar raiders, they were bare-chested, black hair spilling long down their broad backs, and inky markings curling across their chest muscles. Thick, metal-studded belts held their kilts in place, and deadly battle axes hung from them.

I flicked my gaze at another warrior at a standing console. "You have the command deck. Lock onto that ship and get us into position for boarding."

He snapped his heels together and threw his shoulders back. "Yes, Raas."

My battle chief stole a glance at me as we left the command deck and descended a wide staircase, our heavy footfall echoing off the iron and steel that made up our warbird. "You have not led a boarding party in some time, Raas."

"Too long," I said, to halt any more queries into my motivations.

He gave a curt nod, understanding that the matter was not up for further discussion. Although I was a fair Raas, and welcomed my warrior's input, I did not wish to discuss why I wanted to board this insignificant ship personally. I myself did not fully understand.

As we descended farther into the ship, winding through the labyrinth of open-weave, cage-like corridors and pounding down more stairs, my pulse quickened. It had been too long since I had tasted battle, and the anticipation of striking another blow to the Zagrath Empire made my fingers buzz as they rested on the hilt of my axe.

The warriors who walked astride with me had been part of my crew since I took command as the raider horde's warlord, or *Raas*. It had been many rotations since I'd assumed the command after my father, and we had the most victories of any of the other Vandar warlords, but we were still a long way from passing on our battle axes to a new crew. I knew our people's traditions, but I could not imagine ever giving up the life of a raider to live out my days on one of the secret Vandar settlements, far from the empire and the bloody battles that had become as natural to me as breathing.

"What should I tell the rest of the horde?" My majak, Bron, asked.

"Maintain formation and keep weapons trained on the enemy vessel. They may be hiding their capabilities and be more deadly than they appear." I hoped that was the case, my heart beating faster at the thought.

"It is done," he said with a sharp nod, before striding to a console outside the hangar bay and relaying my orders.

My *majak* had ordered a squad of warriors to meet us at the hangar bay, and they were waiting when we strode through the wide doors, their fierce faces just as alight with desire. We all needed a battle. Needed to think we were weakening our enemy. The enemy that seemed to keep coming, no matter how long we fought against it.

When we reached the shuttle ramp, I paused, turning to face my warriors. "All glory to Lokken, god of old."

"Glory to Lokken," my warriors replied, solemnly.

Then I grinned. "Are you ready to slash another hole in the belly of the beast?"

Wide grins spilt their faces as they roared their answer. "For Vandar!"

It had been our war cry for as long as our people had been roaming the wilds of our planet, moving in hordes and battling for control of the land. When we'd been forced to abandon our planet, we had held tight to our traditions. Even now—generations later—our ships traveled in groups of ten or more warbirds, all commanded by a single warlord. We wore the battle clothing of our ancient ancestors and carried their weapons, although we had also developed sophisticated technology for our ships and had phasers attached to our belts, as well as battle axes.

"For Vandar!" The bellows of my warriors reverberated through my own body, making my blood heat and my heart hammer in my chest, as I ran up the ramp to the shuttle with my Vandar brothers close on my heels. We all pulled curved shields off the walls of the ship where they were stored for battle. Bron took the helm while I stood behind, my eyes fixed on the wide opening leading into the blackness beyond.

Gripping the cold steel of the beam overhead, I held tight as the ship rocketed across the hangar bay floor and burst out into space, banking hard and approaching the enemy freighter. The ship looked even more weathered up close, the dull exterior dented and scarred with scorch marks. My lust for battle dampened as I noticed the meager weapons attached to the hull. This was no war ship, I thought, as disappointment choked me.

"Their shields have been disabled, Raas." My first officer twisted his neck to look back at me, his dark brows lifted. "They have issued a surrender."

Low murmuring passed through my warriors, and I

suspected they were thinking what I was—this would not be a battle after all. This was clearly not a ship filled with warriors ready to engage us in battle if they had already surrendered. I doubted its crew were trained warriors, and it was even less probable that this ship had been tasked with moving armaments. The Zagrath would not be foolish enough to trust anything crucial to such a battered old freighter. We were probably preparing to attack a ship carrying blankets and grain.

"Zagrath supplies are still Zagrath supplies," I said, to quell their frustration and my own. "But we will hold our blades unless provoked."

"Working for the Zagrath is provocation enough." Corvak's voice was gravelly.

I agreed, but I also knew that not all under the empire's rule had the freedom we did or the deadly reputation that struck fear in the hearts of anyone who encountered us. Nevertheless, the Vandar raiders were feared because we punished those who stood with the empire. We could not back down or show weakness. Weak warriors did not spend eternity in Zedna with Lokken and the other ancient gods of battle.

"They have surrendered," I said. "But that does not mean they will escape punishment for their alliance with the empire. Blood will be shed for their treacherous act."

Nods and grunts of agreement followed my statement, although I noticed Corvak frown. As was fitting his title, he was only content when engaged in a full-scale battle, and his body boasted the scars to prove it.

Our shuttle jolted as it latched onto the enemy freighter, our docking pincers holding the ship in place as it forced the hangar bay open. I held my breath, part of me hoping the surrender was a ruse and there would be phaser fire as we entered the enemy ship, but the hangar bay was deserted.

We rushed out in a swarm, moving in our practiced formation with shields in front. The ship was not nearly as large as ours, but it was brighter, with amber lights flickering overhead as we moved swiftly down the passageways. I flinched from the unnatural brightness, my eyes adjusting. Why did these aliens like to feel as if they were on a glowing star?

Exposed piping hissed, and the hull seemed to groan without provocation as we moved through the cramped ship. The scent of fuel hung thick in the air, along with the smell of scorched steel, no doubt from the hits they'd taken from us.

I swallowed my disappointment at the sad state of the ship we were taking. No weapons, no warriors. It was almost not worth our time.

"A cargo bay, Raas," one of my warriors said, pointing to a set of doors.

I jerked my head at him and another warrior. "Assess the value and prepare to transport anything worth taking."

"Where are their warriors?" Bron asked, his voice low so only I could hear him as we continued moving. "Is this a trap?"

"I think we both know it is not." My own fingers twitched over my axe, but cold realization was settling hard in my stomach. There would be no battle today.

Ahead a figure appeared then quickly ran ahead and disappeared around a corner.

"A human, not a Zagrath," my *majak* said, disappointment heavy in his voice. Even though the difference was subtle, it was important.

It was rumored that the humanoid Zagrath were

descended from the original people who fled the planet Earth, although they did not call themselves Earthlings now. They'd been part of what had been called the one-percenters. With their sophisticated technology, considerable resources, and even greater greed, these elite humans had dubbed themselves the Zagrath and built an empire, with the mission to colonize and monetize as many planets as possible. They'd also used their wealth to enhance their genetics, so they were slightly larger than humans, with a longer life span. But, they were still no match for the mighty Vandar.

"It matters not," Corvak growled.

But it did. The other humans who populated the galaxy had been desperate escapees from a dying planet, and they did not have the advantages of the Zagrath. Even with only a fleeting glance, I knew that was one of the smaller humans, and the disappointment nearly choked me.

When we reached the doors to their command deck, two of my warriors rushed through first, battle axes held high beside their shields. When I rushed in after them, the war cry that had been on my lips died. Instead of Zagrath soldiers, or even a rough mercenary crew of aliens, there were a handful of humans sitting at consoles, their eyes wide with fear as they watched us storm their command deck. And standing in front of them was a female who looked like she would have liked to kill all of us.

A female. A human female.

Tvek, I cursed to myself at our bad luck. So much for a day of valiant battle.

THREE

Astrid

All the air left my body when the Vandar raiders stormed onto our bridge, their boots pounding so loudly that it drowned out the sound of my own thudding heart.

Crap. They were even bigger than I imagined. It didn't help that they were dressed like some kind of space-age Vikings, with leather and metal the only things covering their massive, bronze bodies corded with muscle. Long, dark tails snapped behind them—the ends tipped with black fur— reminding me that they were definitely not human, although the rest of them seemed pretty human, if not full-on medieval. Even the weapons they brandished looked ancient, and I wondered for a moment how these aliens had managed to terrorize the galaxy. How could a bunch of brutes like this take on the Zagrath Empire and not get blown out of the sky?

Then I remembered that their ships could vanish at will, and were rumored to have impressive firepower. So, they must have been more technologically advanced than they looked. I swallowed hard as my gaze drifted over the long black hair that matched their inky-black eyes and the dark markings etched across their bare chests. If I remembered the rumors I'd heard correctly, Vandar were born with the swirling, black lines, and they had something to do with their mating ritual. I tore my gaze away from them, not wanting to think about these brutes and anything to do with mating. Their unusually large, muscular thighs—displayed through strips of leather worn as some sort of short skirt—were distracting enough.

"Who leads this ship?" One of the raiders stepped forward as he spoke the universal language, and I saw that he was slightly taller and broader than the others, if that was possible. His jaw was square, and his hair brushed back, but loose. He was the only one with a single shoulder covered by a cap of metal armor with a strap crossing his chest, and I assumed he was their leader.

He radiated authority, his feet set wide as he appraised our bridge. He had not drawn his battle axe, but instead tapped his fingers rhythmically on the handle. Even though his muscles were taut, his words were measured.

My sister squared her shoulders. "I'm the captain."

Hearing her voice—strong and steady—made my chest swell with pride. Tara didn't seem to be scared by the raiders at all, even though it was clear they could have killed us all within seconds.

"You?" The Vandar narrowed his glittering eyes at her, and I could not tell if he was amused or offended.

She jutted out her chin. "Yes, me."

"You entered Vandar territory," he said, and this time his voice was little more than a ragged growl. Though low, the sound vibrated through the bridge and made my breath catch in my throat.

Tara didn't flinch. "A mistake we were trying to rectify when your horde chased us down."

The Vandar who was clearly the leader scanned the bridge again, his gaze lingering on me for a moment as his tail swished quickly behind him. I was almost positive he could see that I was shaking. "You work for the Zagrath Empire."

To be aligned with the empire was as good as a death sentence. The Vandar raiders had been fighting a guerrilla war against them for longer than any of us on the bridge had been alive.

Tara shifted from one foot to the other, but did not drop her gaze. "We're an independent freighter. We have no loyalty to the empire."

A muscle ticked in the leader's jaw, and a ripple of movement passed through the other Vandar. Somehow, I knew this was not the right thing to say.

"You only supply their outposts and arm their invaders."

Tara did not respond.

Maybe if she didn't argue back they'd let us go, I thought.

"You think you are innocent of their crimes?" The Vandar leader pressed, his fingers drumming across the hilt of his weapon as he began to pace a tight circle in front of my sister, his head snapping with each turn.

"We aren't Zagrath," Tara repeated, but this time with an edge in her voice. "We made a navigational error. We didn't mean to violate your space."

He stopped pacing and leveled his gaze at her. "A navigational error?"

My stomach clenched. Technically, *we* didn't make an error. I made the error. I sensed Mose's gaze on me, but I didn't look at him.

The Vandar ceased tapping his fingers, and the only thing I could hear was my own uneven breathing. "Error or not, we cannot allow you to continue on your mission to supply our enemy."

Tara grasped her hands behind her. "You can have our cargo."

"I intend to take your cargo. And execute *you*. Your penalty for working for the Zagrath. Let it be a lesson to others who dare support the empire."

There were sharp intakes of breath among our crew. My heart pounded wildly as the reality hit me. My stupidity and lack of focus had sentenced my sister to death—the one person who'd always protected me and looked out for me. My ears started to ring, and black spots danced in front of my eyes.

No no no no no. This wasn't happening. I couldn't lose my sister. She couldn't be executed because of me.

"Executed?" Tara's voice was a low hiss. "For doing a job so we can eat? The Zagrath control everything. How else are we supposed to survive if we don't work for them?"

The Vandar leader swept cold eyes across her. "It is done." Then he scanned the bridge once more and turned to leave.

"You bastard," Tara growled, as she lunged herself toward his retreating back.

I gasped as she was knocked back by one of the other Vandar warriors, who stepped forward to block her from the leader so quickly I barely registered his movement.

One of the raiders towered over my sister, raising his battle axe.

"No!" I screamed, my voice louder than the ringing in my head. "Stop! I should be the one executed."

All eyes swiveled to me, including the leader who'd pivoted back around.

Tara closed her eyes where she lay sprawled on the floor, looking more defeated than she had before.

"It's my fault. I'm the one who made the navigational error. You can't kill my sis...the captain for my mistake. Please," I said, hearing the quaver in my voice. "Kill me, instead."

"No, Astrid," Tara said, her words an order that would have normally made me fall in line.

Not this time.

"You wish me to execute you in her place?" His dark eyes were on me as he crossed the bridge, his long legs eating up the short distance between us so fast that I backed up a few steps, my ass bumping up against a console.

I nodded, ignoring my sister on the floor shaking her head and telling me to shut up. Even though my pulse fluttered, a calm settled over me as the Vandar held my gaze captive with his own. This was the right thing to do. I'd only survived as long as I had because of Tara. She'd been saving my ass for most of my life. It was my turn to save her for a change.

He cocked his head and eyed me up and down unabashedly, his fingers rapping on the hilt of his weapon once more. His tail had stopped swishing and curled up stiffly, the dark tip the only part twitching. He stared at me for so long that my cheeks burned from the scrutiny. I knew at any moment, he would reject my offer and round on my sister again. I met his eyes when they returned to my face, fisting my hands so tightly by my side the nails bit into my flesh. If he was going to kill me, at least I could be brave enough not to look away.

As I locked my gaze on his, my mouth went dry. Instead of being overcome with fear, my pulse fluttered. I'd expected his dark eyes to be cold, emotionless voids, but they were not. They flashed with heat and curiosity, drawing me to him, even as I fought against it.

"Raas?" One of his raiders finally spoke, and I wondered if that was his name.

He jerked his head around, tearing his gaze from mine and darting it over Tara. "Spare her."

A wave of relief coursed through me, even as I braced myself for what would come next.

The Vandar leader turned back to me. "You would die to save your captain?"

"Yes," I said, again holding his deadly gaze as my stomach roiled, the bitter taste of bile burning the back of my throat as fear finally overtook my curiosity. If he was going to kill me, I wished he would hurry up before I humiliated myself by puking all over my own shoes.

"Astrid, no!" my sister cried out. She'd leapt up, but two Vandar held her by the arms to keep her from lunging across the bridge.

He did not turn at my sister's screams, but his pupils flared, making his eyes even blacker. "I have a deal for you, Astrid."

I dropped my gaze to the hand on his weapon, confused as to why he hadn't drawn it. "Deal?"

"Your life for hers."

My confusion deepened. Hadn't that been what I'd already agreed to? Why was he toying with me?

"I will let her live, and your ship can have safe passage out of our sector. But I do not wish to kill you." He leaned so close to my face that I felt the quick inhalation as he seemed to breathe me in. His voice became a low hum that skated down my spine. "You will come with me."

It took me a while to process his words. "Come with you? You aren't going to kill me?"

He gave a faint shake of his head.

Even though I should have felt relief, the hairs on the back of my neck prickled. "I thought the Vandar didn't take prisoners."

"We do not, but I am Raas." His hot gaze traveled down my body again. "I can do what I wish."

From the burning look in his eyes, I knew what he meant. In exchange for my sister's life, I would be expected to pleasure this hulking alien. Cold chills rippled through my entire body, and my heart raced. The thought terrified me, but also sent a thrill through me. A thrill I tried to ignore.

But if that was what he was after, why did he want me? Anyone with eyes could see that my sister was the pretty one. I'd always been the shorter, washed-out version of Tara with too many curves in too many places.

Maybe he didn't want me for the reasons I was thinking. Maybe my imagination was just running away from me again. Maybe he just wanted a servant. Either way, there was no choice but to agree. I managed to bob my head up and down.

He leaned his head close to mine again and took another long breath. "You agree to come with me willingly? I want you to say it."

"I agree," I whispered, even as goosebumps covered my arms.

He straightened and gave me a brusque nod, turning around and calling over his shoulder. "*Vaes!*"

I hesitated, until he looked back at me, speaking in the universal language again. "Come."

My legs were shaky as I followed him, passing my sister, whose eyes were wild.

"What's going on? Where are you taking her?"

I paused in front of her. "It's okay. If I go with him, he'll let the rest of you go."

"Go with him?" Her gaze went to the enormous raider, and she struggled against the two holding her. "No way. You can't take her. I won't let you. She has nothing to do with any of this. I'm the captain. It's my fault."

The one they called Raas cleared his throat, although he did not stop walking off the bridge. "You should come before I change my mind, Astrid."

I threw my arms around Tara even though her arms were being pinned to her side, and I gave her a quick hug. "I'm sorry about everything."

"Don't do this," she begged when I pulled away. "You don't have to do this."

I gave her a small smile, blinking hard to keep the tears pricking the backs of my eyelids at bay. "Yeah, I do."

I turned around, hearing her struggle but forcing myself to follow the massive alien off the bridge without turning around and taking one final look at my sister. I knew if I did, I'd start crying, and the last thing I wanted was for my sister's last memory of me to be of me sobbing like some kind of baby. I didn't meet any of the stares of the other members of the crew, either. I didn't want to see the pity I knew would be etched on their faces. Or maybe it would be relief.

I had to practically run to keep up with the leader's long strides, especially as the rest of the Vandar came up behind me, walking just as quickly as the one they called Raas. There was no sound but the thrum of their boots, like a relentless drumbeat as we moved through the ship. We were walking too fast for me to think about much else, and even my own grief was pushed aside by my attempt to keep pace with them. I paused once we reached the hangar bay and their jet-black shuttle, swallowing hard as I looked at the vessel that would take me away.

As if he sensed my fear, the Raas turned and took me by the arm, propelling me forward and up the ramp before I could think to pull away from him. There were no seats in the ship except for the pilot's, so I was shuffled to the front as the Vandar warriors clutched an iron rail overhead too high for me to reach. Their bodies pressed in, and I could see nothing but them surrounding me.

The ship's engines rumbled to life and it surged forward, the Raas wrapping one arm around me to hold me to him so I wouldn't fall, his tail curling around my legs. It was only when I was cocooned between his thick arm and the firm wall of his body —his heat pulsing into me and making my own skin flush—that the reality of my new life hit me.

I'd made a deal with a Vandar raider. A Raas, no less. One who had complete power over a horde of murderous ships and now over me. I would live the rest of my life—what there was of it—on an alien warship and never see my sister again. Tears rolled hot down my face, the saltiness seeping between my lips.

What had I done?

CHAPTER
FOUR

Kratos

"Engage invisibility shielding and prepare to resume course," I commanded, as we touched down inside our warship.

Bron powered down the shuttle. "Yes, Raas."

I ignored the stares as I led the human down the ramp, flanked by the rest of the boarding party. None of the warriors had uttered a word about me taking the female—not even Bron or Corvak—but I knew they were baffled by my behavior.

There were no females on Vandar raider ships. Only young warriors without mates or families to distract them. Our female needs were met by visits to the hedonistic planets beyond the Zagrath Empire—places where females were free with their affections for coin. Our ships were for battle and nothing else. So why had I violated this tradition and taken the female?

It wasn't like I hadn't been responsible for the deaths of females before. As much as we tried to limit our punishment to Zagrath military, there was always collateral damage. And in a war that had spanned generations and showed no signs of ceasing, there would be much more to come.

"Do you wish us to disable the freighter further?" Corvak asked, his eyes darting down—the only acknowledgment of the female beside me.

I jerked my head quickly. "Leave it. They are no threat. They would not be foolish enough to enter Vandar territory again, and they could not track us even if they did."

The female—Astrid—twitched slightly, but only I felt it. I glanced down at her fair hair, fighting the urge to stroke my hand down it. Only I knew that I would not have killed the female captain. I had wanted to test her courage in the face of death and what her ragtag crew would have done.

I'd wanted to determine how loyal she was to the Zagrath. Instead, this small female had thrown herself at my mercy, and something about her sacrifice had touched me.

Of all those on the command deck of the sad freighter, she had been the last one I would have suspected of such bravery. Even though I surmised that the captain with the fiery hair was her sister, this slight female was clearly not a fighter. Yet she had offered her own life and had not backed down. There was a strength behind the fear. What had surprised me most was my own desire to see more of it. I'd felt drawn to her and the flash of determination behind her green eyes. The sweet curves I had detected beneath her clothing had not hurt, either. Nor had the fact that her scent made my cock hard and my heartbeat quicken.

It had been a long time since I'd felt the thrill I'd experienced when I made the deal with her. My pulse had raced, and blood had rushed hot through my veins, as if I was on a hunt. Even now, my body hummed from the closeness of her as she walked beside me across the flight deck, her footsteps making fast taps on the steel floor. Glancing over, I saw that many of the other warriors were also casting furtive looks at her, their gazes roaming the curves covered snugly by her clothing. Fury flared within me, and my hand went instinctively to my axe before I remembered that the warriors were my own, and I could not fault them for being intrigued by the creature.

Tvek. I uttered the curse in my head. What had I been thinking to bring a prisoner of war aboard my ship? She was right. Vandar did not take prisoners. Only the Zagrath enslaved. We had no brig. To commit an offense worth imprisonment meant being put out an airlock.

I blew out a breath. My decision had been impulsive and foolish—something I would have expected from one of my younger brothers. Not the actions of a seasoned Raas.

She stumbled slightly, and I grabbed her elbow to prevent her from falling. When she chanced a glance up at me, her eyes were rimmed with red and streaks trailed down her cheeks. My gut twisted. I was unused to tears. I pressed my lips together and looked away. Another reason taking her was a mistake.

When we reached the first sprawling metal staircase, Bron eyed me, then her. "Should I take her to…your quarters for you, Raas?"

She trembled next to me as she took in the dark, soaring space of our ship, with stairs crisscrossing overhead in the shadows—a far cry from the well-lit freighter with its curved walls and tight corridors. "I will take her myself and meet you on the command deck."

"But, Raas—"

I cut Corvak off with a flick of my wrist. "You have your orders. I expect to be back on course when I return to the command deck."

My order was followed by sharp clicking of heels, then the loud rattling of the stairs as they started up. Astrid flinched. The echoing sounds of the cavernous warbird must have been an assault to someone used to the steady rumble of a freighter.

I rested a hand on the small of her back, reminding myself that I was much larger than her and considerably more powerful. "*Vaes.*"

"You said that on my ship. What does it mean?" Her voice was soft and shaky, but curious.

"Come," I said, trying to keep my face serious when I saw confusion cross hers. "It means 'come with me.'"

She nodded, moving forward as I led her up the stairs. "You speak the universal language, but still use Vandar?"

I grunted. "Some Vandar words are better."

Another nod, and we walked in silence, winding through the open-weave labyrinth of the ship. Astrid occasionally peered down at the maze of stairs, her grip of the steel handrail making her knuckles pale. We left the stairs and entered a cage-like corridor and finally reached a large, oval-shaped door.

I pressed my hand to a round panel to one side and the gray doors parted in the center, sliding open silently to reveal my private quarters.

"*Vaes,*" I said again, when she paused on the threshold, her pupils flaring as she peered inside.

"This is where...?" She bit her lower lip.

"These are my quarters. This is where you will stay."

She swallowed, nodding and taking a slow step inside.

As much as I wanted to sweep her up and carry her to my huge, round bed, with its headboard made from shields and battle axes welded together, I did not. I let her walk inside on her own, her steps tentative as her gaze swept the space from side to side.

"There is no couch?" she asked finally.

I cocked my head at her. "Couch? I do not know this word."

Her cheeks colored. "Like a place you sit, but wide and long with cushions."

I scanned my living space with its ebony tables and straight chairs. Like most things on my ship, the furnishings were hard and sleek. And as on the rest of the ship, the lighting was dim. "Do you require one of these couches?"

"I thought maybe I could sleep on the couch, so I wouldn't have to kick you out of your bed." She'd turned away from me and was facing the bed, which extended out into the center of the room.

I felt a flash of both amusement and irritation. "You will not be kicking me out of my bed, female. Did you not understand our deal?"

"I wasn't sure…I mean, I thought maybe…"

My heart started to race again, my hunting instincts firing. I came up quickly behind her, winding an arm around her waist and jerking her close to me. I used my tail to circle her legs so she could not kick me. "You do not need to think so much, Astrid." Her breath became quick and shallow. I stroked a finger down her cheek, breathing in her intoxicating scent. "All you need to know is that you are mine now. You belong to a Raas of the Vandar. Your life will be on this ship and with me. In this bed. Do you understand now?"

She moved her head up and down. As I held my hand splayed across her stomach, her rapid heartbeat vibrated into me. Just like prey before it was caught. My cock swelled as she wiggled in my grasp, reminding me how easy she was to overpower, and the tip of my tail quivered in anticipation.

I closed my eyes and inhaled the smell of her hair, resting my chin on it and tucking her into my body as she trembled. Perhaps she understood for the first time that there was no escape. That this was permanent. "Say it."

"Say—?"

"Say that you are mine," I growled. "I need to know that you understand."

She sucked in a ragged breath. "I am yours, Raas."

My own pulse steadied. "You do not need to call me Raas when we are alone. My name is Kratos."

"Kratos," she repeated, as if trying to memorize it.

"Raas is my title. You only need use it when you address me in front of my warriors." I shifted my hand up so that my thumb brushed the swell of her breast.

"What does it mean?"

"Warlord." I whispered into her ear, cupping one breast as she shivered in my arms. She clearly thought I intended to fuck her now. "Although there is nothing I would like more than to bury my cock inside you, I am needed on the command deck. I will not be claiming you now. You can breathe."

Her body relaxed slightly, a sigh leaving her lips. The sound she made almost caused me to rethink my statement. Maybe I had time for a small taste of the female. But before I could move, the ship lurched violently to one side, and we both flew across the room.

CHAPTER
FIVE

Astrid

My ears were ringing as strong hands lifted me off the floor. My leg hurt from where I'd crashed into the corner of a low table, but as soon as Kratos pulled me up, I knew it wasn't broken. Sore? Definitely.

The ship continued to shake, but at least it wasn't sending us flying again. Sirens as deep and sonorous as the Raas' voice echoed overhead and the dim lighting flickered off and on, plunging us into darkness before flaring back on.

"Are you hurt?" Kratos held me by the shoulders, scouring my body with his eyes as unabashedly as he had on my sister's ship.

"I'm fine," I lied. I ached from hitting the table and then the floor, but I wasn't going to whine about it. Not when he'd hit just as hard and seemed unfazed.

His face twisted as he glanced back at the door. "We are clearly under attack. I need to return to the command deck."

Under attack? The sour taste of bile rose again in my throat. I'd been on the Vandar ship for all of ten minutes, and we were already under attack?

He gazed down at me, his hands gripping my arms too tightly. "You must stay here. Do you understand?"

For a moment, I wanted to beg him to stay with me. I wanted to feel his arms wrapped protectively around me again even though I shouldn't have wanted him to touch me. I pushed aside my strange impulse and nodded. Where did he think I was going to run off to on a spaceship, anyway?

"Got it." When he hesitated, I added, "I promise not to go anywhere."

"I will hold you to that promise, female," he growled, and ran out of the room, the doors sliding back together to make a solid oval of metal, with only a faint seam to indicate that it was not a wall. Another hard jolt had me stumbling to the side and landing on the foot of the bed. If a perfectly round bed could have a foot.

It's going to be fine, I told myself. *You're on a Vandar war ship. They're known for being some of the toughest ships in the galaxy. No one ever talks about Vandar ships being blown out of the sky. Do they?*

I gave my head a brusque shake, as if ridding myself of the fearful thoughts crowding my mind. It didn't do any good to be scared. There was absolutely nothing I could do about it. There was nothing I could do about any of it.

Kratos was right. My life was on the Vandar warship now. It had been my decision to take the Raas' deal, and I had to accept it. All of it.

As the ship trembled from what I suspected was more weapons fire, I rubbed my sweaty palms down the front of my dark pants. Part of me had hoped that the Vandar had taken me as a slave, even though I knew his people didn't do that. Even though I'd seen the desire in his eyes, part of me hoped I was wrong. The other part of me I tried to ignore because I knew it was stupid to be attracted to a creature so deadly.

Kratos expected me to sleep with him in this bed, and do plenty more than sleep. I tried to calm my breathing and keep the panic from choking me.

What would happen when he found out that I'd never been with a man—or alien—before? How would he react when he discovered that I wasn't some experienced woman who knew how to pleasure him, but instead, a twenty-year-old virgin, whose total sexual experience consisted of some fumbling kisses and awkward groping?

"Crappity crap!" I wished I could curse as eloquently and vividly as my sister, but the words felt foreign on my tongue. I stood and walked across the glossy, black floors, the movement helping to slow my brain's frantic ping-pong of thoughts. Even though the siren still droned, I began to hum as I walked, holding my fingers in my ear so I could hear the soothing sound.

Since the Vandar didn't take prisoners, I couldn't imagine what they'd do to one who was deemed useless? Would I be put out an airlock, or dropped off alone at some remote outpost? Neither option was appealing. I hummed louder.

Kratos wouldn't discard me. Not after he'd broken his own rules to take me. Right?

"You can do this, Astrid," I told myself. It was the same pep speech I'd given myself so many times over the years, usually before I had to do something I knew I'd be horrible at.

I clenched my fists. This time I didn't have the luxury of

being bad or losing focus. If I wanted to survive, I needed to make this Vandar happy. Whatever that took.

"You don't have to love him," I reminded myself. "Or even like him. You just have to screw him."

That advice sounded eerily close to advice my sister had given me once about holding on to my virginity. She'd thought I needed to just do it so I could move on from the bad, first-time sex to the good stuff. At least that was how she'd put it. Tara didn't have many hang-ups when it came to her sexuality. She didn't have many hang-ups, period. Unlike me. I was basically a bunch of hang-ups held together with body fat.

When I reached the end of the room, my gaze was drawn through a wide arched doorway. Since the siren had stopped sounding, I dropped my fingers from my ears and stepped into a spacious bathroom, almost sighing out loud when I saw the half-moon-shaped, sunken tub to one side.

My sister's freighter only had a handful of shared crew bathrooms, with broken faucets and dodgy water pressure. I'd gotten used to cold showers and hair that never felt thoroughly rinsed, but the sight of the tub filled with steaming water made my heart leap. I didn't know how long it had been since I'd had an actual bath.

Not that this Vandar tub looked like any I'd seen before. The unusually-shaped tub had four different sections—each filled with a different color of water, and each large enough for one or two people to sit in. Steam rose up from the red water at the end, and bubbles covered the surface of the orange water next to it. The green water was too opaque to see through, but the blue water at the other end was crystal clear.

I glanced behind me at the arched doorway to the room beyond. Kratos was busy on the bridge, and I didn't expect him to come running back right away, even though the ship was no longer shaking. He was busy with his duties as warlord, and I was going to take advantage of his absence.

Acting quickly before I could change my mind, I peeled off my clothes and left them in a neat pile on the black-stone counter. I gave another furtive glance around me, glad that no one could see me dipping a toe in the blue water, completely naked.

I almost yelped from the cold sting, pulling my toe out just as quickly as I'd lowered it in. "Who sits in water that cold?"

The Vandar Raas, obviously, although I guessed soaking in ice water wasn't close to the toughest thing the huge alien did. I shivered, not from the cold water, but from the memory of his hard muscles pressed up against me. And the very hard and very large thing I'd felt on my ass when he'd held me to him on the shuttle.

I moved to the green water, forcing myself not to think of how large the Raas was, as I dipped my foot cautiously into the murky water. It wasn't freezing, but it wasn't warm, either. It was the same temperature as the room, but the water itself was viscous, my foot slick on the bottom when I pulled it out.

Moving to the bubbling orange water, I was pleased to find it warm. I sat on the edge and dropped down into the pool, my toes reaching the bottom when the water was over my breasts. Now that my face was closer to the water, I could smell a warm, spicy scent emanating from the bubbles as they broke the surface. There was nothing feminine about the perfumed water, but inhaling it made my shoulders relax and my mind drift.

Memories came flooding in.

I was on Parnisi III with Tara. It was after our parents had been killed, but before she'd won the freighter. We were huddled around a table in the back of a bar that had long since passed "seedy."

She'd motioned to a crust of bread left on a plate from the last occupants of the table, a bone picked white next to it. "Eat."

I'd eyed it, starving but not willing to eat the only scrap we'd seen all day. "We should share it."

She shook her head. "You need it more."

I'd felt the gentle rebuke, but was too hungry to care much. She was right. I hadn't taken to deprivation like she had. Tara had gotten sinewy and lean over the past months. I had miraculously not lost my curves, as I'd gotten weaker and weaker.

She'd pushed the crust toward me—the plate leaving a trail of grease across the grimy, wood table—then her gaze had settled on a well-dressed male sitting by himself, and her jaw had hardened. "Don't worry. I know how to get more."

I shook my head, forcing the memory to fade. Tara had always done whatever it took to survive—for both of us to survive. I hoisted myself over the barrier between the sections and slipped into the red water, flinching slightly from the heat, but welcoming the pain. Although my skin burned for a moment as it adjusted, I let out a moan as the water covered me up to my chin.

I thought of my sister's face as I'd hugged her for the last time. I hoped I would be able to forget the look of shock and betrayal. I even preferred remembering her rolling her eyes at me to the pain in her eyes before I'd turned from her. She hadn't understood. How could she? She'd always been the one to sacrifice. No one had ever sacrificed for her. Not until that moment.

I inhaled the hot steam. It didn't hold the scent of the

bubbling water, but it warmed my nose and tickled the length of my throat. Resting my head on the stone ledge, I let the water wash away all the regret and pain of the day. Regret that I'd been the reason my sister had nearly been executed, and the pain of losing her after all. Even though I was on a Vandar warbird and was now the property of its menacing warlord, at the moment, my sister was safe, and I was content.

I hummed as I bobbed in the water, the high notes echoing off the stone walls and reminding me of my mother who used to sing all the time. Tara had forbidden me to sing after our parents had died, so I'd learned to hum quietly to myself instead. Sometimes humming was the only thing that could calm me.

Once my fingers started to wrinkle, I stopped humming and lifted myself out of the steaming pool, casting my eyes around for a towel. Nothing. Did the Vandar drip-dry? That didn't seem practical, and no way was I going to leave puddles all over the slick floors or put my dry clothes back on while I was soaking wet.

I eyed the open shower at the other end of the bathroom and all the flat buttons inset in the black-stone walls. Maybe one of them was for drying?

Padding over, I inspected the buttons and the various nozzles overhead and imbedded in the walls. None of them were in any language I could read, the symbols completely foreign to me.

"Here goes nothing," I muttered to myself as I pressed a button.

Instead of drying me as I'd hoped, a torrent of water gushed from overhead. I yelped and tried to find the button again, but the water had drenched my head and was streaming into my eyes. It was pleasantly warm, though, and the hard flow felt good on my shoulders. I stood under it, turning so it could pound on all parts of my back and stretching my arms high over my head, the rush of water as it hit the stone floor drowning out any other noise, even my own loud humming.

I finally found the button to stop the water, spluttering and wiping at my eyes. When I opened them, I saw him standing in the doorway, watching me. His face betrayed nothing, but his pupils had dilated so much they shone as obsidian as the stone around me.

CHAPTER
SIX

Kratos

I heard the torrent of water the moment I stepped into my quarters, my eyes raking the room and not finding her. My flash of panic faded when I realized that she was bathing and then my body tingled with anticipation that the small female was preparing herself for me. It had been a while since we had visited a pleasure planet, and my fist made a poor substitute for a willing female.

I unhooked my shoulder armor and left it on a stand next to the door, along with my weapons. I should not have any more use for them at the moment. Although the Zagrath ship had arrived quicker than I'd expected, it had not been able to follow us for long, once we'd activated our invisibility shielding. The damage they'd done before we'd gone dark had been minimal, although it had felt like the ship had been tearing apart. Our shields had held, and repairs to the impacted hull were underway. As were we, to the far end of the Carborian sector to resupply.

I kicked off my boots and crossed to the bathing chamber, hearing her before seeing her. The human was humming as she stood under the flow of water, her high notes bouncing off the slick stone and filling the space. I could not remember the last time I'd heard a female's voice like that, and I was so distracted by the sound that I did not focus on her body right away.

When I did turn my attention to her naked form, water rushing down her pale skin and darkening her light hair, my mouth went dry. She was tiny, that I already knew, but her slight stature did not mean she was small everywhere. I'd already felt her softness when I'd held her earlier, but even as I got only a side view, all her curves were on display for me— her high, round breasts and her flared hips, the gentle curve of her belly and her full ass. My cock stiffened instantly, tenting my battle kilt.

Tvek. I'd never seen a female I wanted to bury my cock in as much as I did this one.

She fumbled on the wall, and I fought my instinct to step in and turn off the water for her. But I didn't. I waited, watching her as she swiped the droplets off her face and opened her eyes. Her lips parted slightly when she saw me, and she stopped moving, her hands going still by her face. Her gaze drifted down, then her eyes grew wide when she saw my cock straining against my uniform.

I reached behind my waist and unfastened the belt. My kilt loosened and dropped to the floor with a soft thud. Vandar did not wear anything under our battle kilts, as was tradition, and we covered as little of our skin as was necessary. I knew this was not a trait that humans shared.

"What are you...?" She took a step back and hit the wall,

activating one of the side nozzles that shot a fine spray of icy mist at her from two sides. She gasped at the sudden cold, her attention drawn from me to the walls and the buttons she did not understand.

I reached her in a couple of long strides, turning off the mist, but not before being covered in the fine spray myself. I looked down and saw that she'd wrapped her arms over her chest and was rubbing them briskly. I reached for her hip to pull her to me, but she flinched from the touch, her face registering pain instead of fear.

Glancing at her skin, I saw that her hip wore an angry bruise. "You're hurt."

"I think it's from when I hit the table earlier. When we fell." Her voice shook as she stared straight ahead at my chest. "I didn't notice it until you…"

I cursed myself and dropped my hand, thinking how big and rough it looked next to her soft skin. Skin that was now mottled purple and red.

"It's fine," she said, her voice shaking a little less. "I bruise easily, and I'm a total klutz. I'm always falling or bumping into things. It will go away in a few days."

I frowned and stepped away from her. It did not look like it would fade quickly. It looked painful and tender, like blood was pooling under the surface. Of course, I'd had much worse, but I also had never had skin so soft or unmarred. As far as I could see, she had no scars or marks from combat. Only the damage she'd sustained when she'd come onto my ship.

This was a mistake. This is why we do not have females on warbirds. I had not heard my father's voice in a while, but it had been my constant companion for many astroyears. I emitted a low growl, as if warning him to stay away. I did not need him telling me what to do any longer. He was gone, and I was Raas.

I spun on my heel and left the bathing chamber, willing my father's voice to leave me. I did not need him to tell me that I should not show her kindness. I knew what he would have said about sparing her life and bringing her on board. He would have thought me weak. According to him, a Vandar Raas must show no mercy, and certainly not to a human who had dared to violate Vandar law. He had shown no mercy when he'd trained me, and I had the mended bones to prove it.

"You are not here," I whispered to the air as I crossed naked to the door and pressed the communication panel beside it, barking orders to my first mate.

But my father had gotten his wish. I was merciless. At least that was what was said of me. I did not spare lives or hesitate to deliver punishment. Until now.

"Vaes!" I bellowed, turning toward the bathing chamber.

She appeared in the arch, her arms still covering her breasts as she dripped water in puddles around her feet and her bundle of dirty clothes tucked under one arm.

I walked to a high cabinet and opened a drawer, retrieving two lengths of buff-colored, tightly woven cloth, wrapping one around my waist and taking the other to her.

"Leave those." I motioned to her clothes. "They will be no use to you here."

She blanched and didn't drop them.

I tempered my gruff voice. "Vandar females do not wear such tight leg coverings."

She tipped her head up to meet my eyes. "I'm not a Vandar female."

Irritation flared within me and my tail snapped from side to side. I was not used to being contradicted. "You are still

41

mine, and I do not wish any other male seeing the shape of you." My heart pounded as I let my gaze fall lower. "It is only for my eyes." I snapped my head back up and steeled my voice. "Do you understand?"

She nodded and let the clothes fall to the floor. I wrapped the cloth around her, my fingers skimming her skin and buzzing from the touch. When the fabric reached from under her arms to her ankles, I rolled the top down several times until it held.

She peered down at the column of cloth. "You want me to wear this?"

I pressed my lips together to keep from smiling. "No. This is for drying. I will have clothes brought for you."

Before she could ask more, I scooped her into my arms and carried her to the bed. She didn't make a noise, but her body stiffened.

"Do not worry." I lay her on one side of the bed that dwarfed her, and I straightened. "I have no intention of claiming you tonight."

Even though the wrinkles in her brow smoothed, she tilted her head at me. "But I thought..."

I nodded to her hip. "You are injured. I am not such a brute that I would cause you more pain." I leaned down and let my lips brush her ear. "Because when I do take you, I do not promise I will be able to go slow or be gentle."

I felt the quick intake of breath followed by a warm huff of air on my neck. It was enough to make me want to rip off the cloth and bury my cock in her, no matter her injury. I closed my eyes and breathed in the scent of her as my cock swelled again, willing myself to control my urges and banishing the voice reminding me that I needed to take before it was taken from me.

Then I heard the pounding on the door.

CHAPTER
SEVEN

Astrid

I tried not to whimper as he leaned so close to me that the hard planes of his chest brushed my skin. Even though he'd said he wouldn't claim me because I was hurt, I didn't believe him. Not when he was so close to me and so hard all over.

I couldn't stop thinking about his massive cock—rising thick and long from his body with the same dark, curling lines marking it that marked his chest—and imagining what something that huge would feel like for my first time. A baptism by fire, my sister would have called it. Not that it would have terrified her. Nothing scared her, unlike me.

Kratos seemed to have no shame at being naked in front of me. Even if I'd stared directly at his cock, I doubt he would have cared. Still, looking at it while he'd crossed the bathroom had made my pulse skitter and my legs turn to jelly, so I'd kept my gaze anywhere but there.

When someone started to knock loudly on the door, he jerked up, and I allowed myself a long exhale.

"*Vaes!*" His voice boomed across the hard surfaces of the room.

I propped myself up on my elbows. The door slid open and a Vandar warrior stepped inside, clicking his heels together when he saw the Raas standing next to the bed.

"Is that her?" he asked, although the question seemed unnecessary, and he didn't wait for an answer to move forward, shifting the leather bag that hung across his shoulder so that it was in front of him.

Kratos pulled the fabric covering me, so that one leg was exposed, and I swatted at his hand without thinking. Both Vandar males stopped moving, and the air in the room seemed to still.

"What are you doing?" I asked, holding my hand over the one Kratos still clutched to my fabric covering.

He drew in a long breath, his dark eyes sparking as he held my gaze. "Allowing the healer to see your injury." His voice was low, but brimmed with impatience. "Would you rather risk internal bleeding?"

I wanted to tell him that I seriously doubted I had internal bleeding, but my leg did ache, and the color of the bruise had quickly shifted from red to blue to deep purple.

"I can do it," I said, shifting the cloth so that it revealed my bruise, but not *everything* from the waist down.

Kratos grunted but released his grip. "You humans are afraid to show your skin."

"You're the one who doesn't want me to wear pants because they're too tight," I snapped back. "What happened to not wanting any other male to see me?"

An exasperated sigh. "Vaaton is not any other male. He is our healer. Now, do you want him to take care of your injury?"

I stole a glance at the Vandar who hadn't moved since we'd started our exchange. His eyes darted between us, and he didn't seem to know what to do. Although he wore the same leather skirt that the rest of the warriors did, his expression was less fearsome, and he carried fewer scars on his exposed skin. Even his tail didn't snap back and forth like those of the other Vandar.

I released my own impatient breath. "Fine."

Kratos stepped back and waved the healer forward. "She hit herself on the corner of the table when our ship was impacted."

The Vandar he'd called Vaaton knelt by the bed, narrowing his eyes at the bruise that was getting darker and darker. He placed his fingers on it, and I bit my bottom lip at the sharp pain. He made a noise in the back of his throat before removing a small, metal device from his bag and running it over my mottled skin. He studied the device for a moment, then gave a curt nod, as if to himself. "A deep bruise with some bleeding, but nothing broken. I will give her an injection to speed the healing and help with the pain."

"An injection?" I sat up further. I hated needles.

The healer ignored me as he returned the device to his bag and took out a flat, steel box. He placed it next to me on the bed, popping it open to reveal a long syringe.

A wave of nausea made me flop back on the bed and suck in a deep breath. "How is it you have technology that can make ships disappear and scanners that can see if a bone is broken or not, but you're still using needles like that? Are you really the sadists everyone says you are? Is that it?" I opened my eyes and saw Kratos standing with his arms folded over his chest, clearly unconcerned by my outburst. "You love to inflict pain, so you blow up ships and execute innocent people and…" A sharp sting in my hip made me yelp and look down at Vaaton, who was calmly putting away the syringe. "…use darn huge needles!"

Kratos blinked at me. "Darn?"

I ignored him. The Vandar probably had all sorts of filthy curse words, and he no doubt used them all the time —another reason Tara would have been a better pick for him.

The healer stood and faced Kratos. "She will be fine. I added a sedative to the injection, so she can get some rest." He paused and gave the Raas a meaningful look. "And so can you."

"Sedative?" I pushed myself back up on my elbows. I wanted to be outraged that the alien had drugged me, but I was already relaxing—an enticing oblivion not far from reach.

Focusing on the Raas, I saw that the cloth he'd wrapped around his waist had slipped down so that the deep V-cuts on either side of his corded stomach were exposed. A pulse of heat throbbed between my legs, and I let out a breathy sigh.

Both aliens swung their heads toward me.

"Perhaps I was mistaken, Raas," the healer said, one eyebrow lifting.

I could have sworn I saw the corner of Kratos' mouth twitch, but he only nodded once before the Vandar backed out of the room.

I blinked heavily as I let myself sink back onto the bed. "This isn't fair. I don't want to…"

His stance relaxed once the door had shut, and it was only the two of us. He sat next to me, tugging the fabric back over my leg. "I have told you I will not touch you before you heal."

"So, it's a promise?" My words were slurred, and he appeared fuzzy around the edges. I reached out one hand and took hold of something soft. That felt nice. I stroked it between my fingers until I heard the raider make a choked noise.

I glanced down. Crap. I was holding the tip of his tail, which even though wet, was like spun silk. His expression was tight, but he stood ramrod straight. I dropped his tail immediately, warmth rushing to my cheeks.

His jaw relaxed, but a vein still throbbed in the side of his neck. "You are mine to do with as I like, human. You gave yourself to me. I do not owe you a promise." His voice rasped low before softening. "But I will give you one, just the same. A Raas does not break his word."

"Raas Kratos," I murmured, humming to myself. Why did I like the sound of his name so much? Why did it feel comforting to repeat it to myself like a mantra? Everything about the alien should have terrified me, but instead I felt pulled to him.

He studied me, his brows pressed together. "Yes, I am Raas. And you are mine."

"I am your what?" My eyes were heavy as I fought to stay awake, but tears stung the backs of my eyelids. "Your war prize? Your whore?"

"No." His voice was sharp.

I moved my head up and down sluggishly. "I guess a virgin can't really be a whore, anyway."

Even through the haze of the sedation, I could see the change on his face as he computed the word, his jaw clenching.

My chin quivered, although I didn't know why I was

suddenly on the verge of tears again. Why did I care so much if I disappointed him? "I guess I'm not what you expected, huh?"

My eyes fluttered closed, but I could still hear him.

"No, you are not, Raisa."

"Astrid," I whispered. "My name is Astrid."

He brushed something down my cheek, and I suspected it was the velvety tip of his tail. "When you wake, Raisa, we will discover why you draw me to you like a *carvoth* to a flame, won't we?"

I desperately wanted to stay awake, to ask what *raisa* meant and hear more of this warlord's thoughts when he thought no one was listening. But the Vandar sedative worked quickly, and soon I'd slipped away from his gentle caress and into a deep sleep, my own humming the last sound I heard.

CHAPTER
EIGHT

Kratos

All eyes turned toward me when I entered the command deck, heels clicked, then my warriors returned to their tasks. All but Corvak, who walked up to stand next to me and face the wide view of space stretching across the front of the command deck.

We stood together silently as the consoles hummed and our sensors emitted low beeps. Our speed was steady, and the floor vibrated from the throaty rumble of the engines. I was glad to be back on my command deck where the sounds and smells were familiar, and far away from the soft, sweet-smelling female who confused me so.

When she'd stroked my tail, I thought I would lose control, but I'd reminded myself that she did not know the tip of Vandar tails were so sensitive. If she'd known that stroking my tail was almost as arousing as stroking my cock, she would not have done it. I knew that, but it was hard to remember just how much she didn't know about my kind. It was going to be very difficult to keep my promise, and I wondered—not for the first time—why I'd made it to her in the first place.

Even though he did not look at me, Corvak's disapproval pulsed off him in waves. Of anyone, it would be my battle chief who would be the most threatened by my actions. And I'd always known that Corvak was a beast who attacked when threatened.

"No trace of the Zagrath in pursuit?" I asked before he could speak.

"None, Raas." He cleared his throat. "They would not come at all, if we had destroyed that freighter."

I knew he was right, but I did not like the reminder of my weakness. Although we were kin, I was still his Raas. I swiveled my gaze at him, watching a muscle twitch in the side of his face. "You question my judgment?"

"Never before, Raas."

Heat threatened to suffuse my face. *Never before.*

"But now you challenge your Raas?" I heard the fury beneath my carefully modulated words, and watched his jaw drop slightly. He knew he'd gone too far.

Corvak turned to face me as bodies shifted around us, and heads turned with interest. "You know I would never challenge you. I have served under you for as long as you have commanded this horde."

I clasped my hands behind my back, aware that my warriors were watching and hearing every word. "Maybe you think you know better now? Maybe you think me weak?"

"Never." Corvak's scarred face was earnest as he held my

eyes. "You have killed more Zagrath than any Raas before you except for—"

"My father," I finished for him, turning away. "But I have spilled enough enemy blood for you not to doubt my reasons, Corvak. If I spared that worthless freighter, I had my reasons. Ones I do not need to share with anyone, not even my battle chief."

"Yes, Raas." The heat had seeped out of his voice. "I did not know that sparing the humans was part of your strategy."

"Sometimes it is important to confuse our enemy." I knew our enemy was not the only one I had baffled with my actions, but I was in no mood to explain myself to my crew. Not when I myself did not fully understand why I did what I did.

"Of course, Raas."

"Do you anticipate any more encounters on our way to the Carborian sector?" I asked, cutting off discussion of the earlier events.

"Long-range sensors show no enemy ships or outposts on our way."

"Good." I shifted my weight. "We are overdue to restock our rations and fuel stores."

Corvak cleared his throat. "I would like to request a stop on Jaldon."

My pulse quickened, then stuttered to a stop. Jaldon. One of the pleasure planets that welcomed Vandar raiders with open arms—and much more.

I immediately sensed a change in the energy of the command deck. This had already been discussed before my battle chief had broached it with me. Not surprising. We often stopped at Jaldon when we were on a supply run. I usually partook as eagerly as any of my warriors, enjoying the strong drinks and the easy females.

But now, I hesitated. Did I want to leave my new female to pleasure myself with a whore? Then again, I had yet to taste my female, and I'd given her my word that I would not until she was healed. Perhaps I needed to release tension as much as the rest of my men.

"Raas?" Corvak prodded.

"A stop on Jaldon is well-deserved," I said, raising my voice so all on the command deck could hear. "It is done."

A low rumbling of pleasure passed through my warriors as I uttered the Vandar phrase that meant I had made a final decision, and I allowed myself a small smile. It *was* well-deserved. We had been on our current raiding run for too long—intercepting transports and invading Zagrath outposts —and it was past time for us to enjoy the spoils of war.

"Thank you, Raas." Corvak clicked his heels with a snap before returning to his standing console.

I gave a final visual sweep of the command deck, satisfied that we were flying safely hidden from our enemy, and my eyes lingered on the view screen displaying the dark expanse, pinpoints of light flickering. As much as I was used to life in space, I would be glad to set our ship down on solid ground and have dirt beneath my feet and sunlight on my back. I felt a pang for the wide plains of the home world I'd never seen, wondering what it would be like to lead a horde of warriors thundering across the land instead of the cold sky.

I gave a shake of my head and strode off the command deck, only realizing that Bron was behind me when I'd reached the first iron staircase. I twisted to face him.

"How is she? I heard you called the healer."

"Bruised in the attack," I said. "Nothing Vaaton couldn't fix."

He nodded, but his gaze dropped.

"What is it, *majak*? Do you come to question my judgement, too?"

His gaze jerked to mine. "Never. My only concern is for you, Raas."

"For me?" I almost laughed. "You think the small female a danger to me? Maybe you did not get a good look at her."

He inclined his head at me, not smiling. "I got a good look at the way *you* looked at her."

My throat tightened. Bron had always been able to see into me where others could not. It was why he was my *majak*, my most trusted advisor and warrior. "You think the way I... You think she will make me weak?"

"There is a reason we do not bring females onto our warbirds," he said, not answering my question. "They are a distraction."

"Maybe I need a distraction." I bit out the words. "Maybe I have been killing and chasing so long I need something to fill my mind aside from memories of war cries and the smell of blood."

"She will do this for you?"

I did not know what the human would do, but I knew I'd seen something in her that drew me in and made me want to know more. Perhaps she was only a distraction, but she was a desirable one. And I knew all the things I wished to do to her. "She will fill my bed, at least."

Bron cut his gaze to me. "If that is all she will do, Raas."

I tamped down my ire as I felt it flare inside me. I knew Bron was not challenging my authority as Raas, or questioning my judgement. It was why he'd stepped off the command deck with me and why he kept his voice low. I could not be angry with my *majak* for his concern. We had fought too long side by side.

"You know that is all she can do." My eyes went to the

marks on his chest and then to mine—our mating marks. Only when I'd found my one true mate would the marks expand across my arms and down to my stomach and appear on the female's skin, as well. It had never happened with a female who was not Vandar before.

He exhaled, his relief evident. Even though he was relieved, the reminder that she would only ever be a distraction made my stomach clench. But I had known that when I'd taken her, and I had not cared.

I clapped him on the shoulder. "I will join you on Jaldon, and you will see how the female holds no sway over me."

His dark eyebrows arched. "Yes, Raas."

CHAPTER
NINE

Astrid

I stretched my arms overhead and sighed, surprised when my fingers didn't touch the hard, steel wall of my rack. Our freighter didn't have space for private quarters—except for a small cabin for the captain—so I slept in the stacked racks that were so tight I couldn't sit up without hitting my head and couldn't extend my arms overhead without hitting the wall. At first, the cramped space had made me claustrophobic, and I'd kept the privacy curtain open while I slept, but eventually I'd grown used to it.

I rolled over, the silky sheets slipping over my bare skin. Silky? That made me blink myself awake. The sheets on our ship were rough, and I never slept naked.

The high, dark ceiling loomed over me, and I tipped my head back to see the headboard of iron shields and curved axes welded together. I was definitely not on my sister's freighter anymore.

The Raas's quarters were silent and much as I remembered them—sparsely furnished, and dimly-lit with black, reflective floors. One thing I had not remembered was the fire that crackled in a fireplace inset in the far wall. That had not been burning when I'd arrived, although I welcomed it since the room itself was cold.

Sitting up, I wrapped the soft, black sheet around myself. When had I gotten under the covers, and where had my towel gone? The last thing I remembered was getting a shot and falling asleep as the Raas talked to me.

I pressed my lips together. It wasn't hard to imagine that he'd been the one to remove the towel and put me to bed. I suppose I was lucky that was all he'd done, although I recalled him making a promise not to touch me until I'd healed. Tugging up the sheet, I peered down at my bruise.

"Amazing," I whispered, running my fingers over the skin that was now pink instead of swollen and furiously purple. Whatever the healer had given me, had really worked. I guessed fancy weapons and cool tech weren't the only things the Vandar had developed.

I swiveled my head, taking in the entire room and listening for sounds other than the popping of the fire. When I was certain I was alone, I stood and crossed to the fireplace, dragging the sheet with me.

I held one hand at a time to the fire—using the other to keep the sheet wrapped around me—letting the blue flames warm my fingers. It was clearly an artificial fire, but the dancing flames still mesmerized me. I hummed to myself as I watched them, trying to think of anything but the reality of where I was.

Not that I knew where I *actually* was. The Vandar warbird

had taken us who knew how far from where I'd been, and I had no clue how long I'd been sleeping. Although, from the heaviness in my head and the ache in my stomach, I suspected I'd been out for a while.

Inhaling deeply, I smelled something savory that was not coming from the fire. Food. I peered around the room again, this time my gaze catching on some plates and bowls on one end of the long table. I didn't waste any time hurrying over, lifting the clear domes covering the food and keeping it warm. I pulled a cloth off the top of a bowl to reveal knots of bread, the yeasty scent wafting up.

I almost moaned out loud. That's what I'd been smelling —freshly baked bread. I took a bite of one of the pieces, closing my eyes to savor the taste. I hadn't had fresh bread in longer than I could remember. On my sister's freighter, we survived on protein powders and ration packs.

I swallowed and took another eager bite then washed it down with the ruby-red liquid that filled a chunky, metal goblet. Some sort of wine, but with a kick. I'd have to be careful with that, I thought, putting the goblet back on the table.

"You are awake."

His deep voice made me jump, almost dropping the sheet as I spun around to face him entering the room. I'd been so busy wolfing down food that I hadn't even heard the door slide open.

I nodded, pulling the silky fabric back up as the Raas watched me. "I just woke up." I glanced down at the bowl of bread. "Thank you for the food."

He wore his shoulder armor again, but there were smudges of dirt and streaks of dark red across his bare chest. "I'm glad you ate. You have been out for a full cycle."

"You mean a day?" I rubbed a hand to my forehead. "I've been asleep for a whole day?"

He shrugged, walking toward me with long strides. "If that is what humans call it, then yes, you have been asleep for a day. It is normal. Healing makes you tired." He tilted his head at me when he'd reached me. "You are healed, are you not?"

Panic fluttered in my chest, and I leaned my head back to look up at him. "It's much better."

His gaze moved down to my leg draped in the black sheet, and I realized I was holding my breath. He grunted and twisted his body to one side, nodding his head at his armor. "I need you to remove this for me."

I let out my breath, dropping my gaze to the leather buckle across his broad back. It was clear I'd need two hands to unhook it, so I tucked the sheet up under my armpits and attempted to hold the slippery fabric in place while my fingers worked the buckle. His bronze skin was softer than I'd expected, and my fingertips lingered once I'd unhooked the straps, pressing gently against his muscle, the velvety skin a stark contrast to the rigid hardness beneath.

I'd never been so close to someone so huge or so deadly. I paused when I felt his eyes on me, my fingers jerking back as if scorched. "Sorry."

"You do not need to apologize for touching me," he husked.

I turned my attention back to my work, my cheeks burning. Since the straps hung freely, I attempted to lift the metal shoulder cap, but it was heavier than I'd expected and my arms lifted quickly to keep it from crashing to the floor, which meant that the sheet slipped down and pooled around my feet.

I stood completely naked, holding the heavy armor with

both hands as he turned back around. I was too terrified to drop the shoulder cap for fear I'd break my foot or his. I wasn't sure if my arms were shaking from the weight or the fear, but I knew I couldn't hold it for much longer.

Raas Kratos didn't lower his eyes from my face as he took the armor from me. "Thank you, Raisa."

I hurriedly snatched the sheet from the floor and wrapped it around myself as he turned and walked back to the stand next to the door, hanging his armor with his weapons. He slid his feet out of his boots, unhooked his wide belt, and let his kilt fall to the floor. It was not the first time I'd seen him naked, but it was the first long look I'd gotten of his bare ass as he walked to the bathroom.

It was true I hadn't seen many bare asses, but I was one-hundred-percent sure I'd never seen one as fine as his. Normally, I would have been distracted by his swishing tail, but it was seeing his cock swinging between his legs from behind that made my heart stutter in my chest.

I blew out a breath to steady myself and walked back to the table. At least he was in there, and I was out here. The more distance between me and the scary warlord, the better. I took a gulp of wine, welcoming the sharp kick as I swallowed.

"*Vaes,*" he called out, his voice reverberating off the stone of the smaller room.

By now, I knew what that Vandar word meant. I suspected that whatever he wanted from me in there was better than what would happen if I disobeyed. I walked quickly across the room, stopping in the arched doorway.

The Raas sat in the red water, his arms folded on the ledge and his head resting on them. His eyes were closed, and his black hair was wet across his back. "You will wash me."

I glanced around the room for a cloth or a sponge or something with a long handle. Of course, there was nothing.

"With your hands, Raisa," he said, as if reading my mind.

There was that word again. I wanted to know what it meant but I was afraid it was the Vandar equivalent of "servant girl. Or worse, "bonehead."

I went to the edge of the sunken pool and knelt next to him, holding my sheet with one hand while scooping hot water onto his exposed back with the other.

After a few moments, he opened one eye. "Get in." Then he added, "Without the sheet."

Great, I thought. Just great.

This is what you signed up for, Astrid, the critical voice in my head reminded me. *You knew you'd be attending him in some way. So, pull on your big-girl panties and get in the darn water.*

"I'm going, I'm going," I whispered to myself, my cheeks heating when he opened his eyes again and furrowed his brow. Sometimes I really wished my inner voice knew how to curse.

I moved to the other end of the pool, dropping the sheet and slipping into the water as fast as I could. His huge body took up most of the space, but I managed to slide to one side of him. I sucked in my stomach so as not to touch his body, and carefully splashed water across his back. The streaks of brown and red dissolved into the already-crimson water, and I only had to rub at a few tenacious spots to remove it all.

He lay completely still in the water while I worked, his breathing deep and steady. He only shifted when my fingers feathered across one of the scars on his back.

"So why are you so dirty?" I asked, my curiosity finally overcoming my desire for him not to notice me. "Did I miss a battle while I was asleep?"

"Not much of one." He twisted his head to face me and rested it on his arms again. "A new Zagrath military outpost on Gurlaatia Prime."

My hands stilled on his back. "You attacked it?"

"We removed the Zagrath from a planet that is not theirs."

"By killing a bunch of Zagrath soldiers?" I thought of the blood I'd washed off him and the fact that there were no wounds on his body.

He opened his eyes. "They are invaders."

"Who conscript a bunch of innocent people to fight for them."

He lifted his head, his eyes sparking. "They are not innocent, if they fight for the empire."

"The Zagrath will just send another bunch of soldiers to the outpost."

The Raas turned over in the water, sitting up until his naked body brushed against mine. "Then we will kill them, as well."

I huffed out a breath. "Until what? Until you kill everyone in the galaxy? When does it end?"

He spun me around so quickly, I screamed. He cupped my body with his own and braced me between him and the wall of the pool with one large palm spread across my belly. I'd been wrong to think he was relaxed, as his cock was thick and hard and pressing against my ass cheeks.

"It ends when I say it ends, Raisa," he murmured into my ear, the words vibrating down my spine. "Or maybe you'd rather it was my blood being spilled? That way you would not have to fulfill your end of our bargain?"

I shook my head without speaking.

"If you do not wish to be mine," he said, nipping at the skin on my neck as his tail curled around me and the wet tip stroked my bare sex, "I could always hunt down that little ship of your sister's again."

I gritted my teeth, hating that his touch made my heart race and my nipples harden. I despised the fact that my body desperately wanted to surrender to him while the rational part of me wanted to slit his throat. I parted my legs, fixing my eyes on the wall as his tail moved between my thighs. "I will not go back on our deal."

CHAPTER
TEN

Kratos

The blood roared in my ears as she opened her legs to me. The heat of the water had made me almost lightheaded, as had my desire for her. Pressing against her soft, small body, it was all I could do to keep myself from impaling her with my cock from behind while my tail stroked her from the front.

I slid my hand up from the swell of her belly and palmed one of her round breasts, circling the hard point with my thumb. She arched into me but did not make a sound.

Even though I had never been with a human female, I'd heard about them. I knew where their pleasure centers were, and what to do to make them respond the way I wanted. I liked my fucking just like I preferred my battles—loud and fierce.

Bending her forward at the waist, I dragged the crown of

my cock through her folds, hesitating when I thought about what she'd said as she'd been drifting under the sedation. She was untouched, which meant that this would hurt her. Looking down at her small frame dwarfed by my larger one, I wondered if she'd be able to take all of me.

I hesitated, then gave my head a hard shake. *You are a Raas and she is your captive. She is yours to take, so take her.*

My tail moved up the swell of her belly until the wet tip circled one of her nipples. I knew she liked the feel of my silken fur on her from the way the flesh pebbled, and the sensation of her bumpy flesh against the tip of my tail made my cock throb. Lowering my head to her neck, I stroked my cock back and forth between her folds. I already knew that she had nothing but a narrow strip of fine hair at the top of her sex. I had seen as much when I'd put her in bed, but I hadn't expected the skin of her folds to be so velvety smooth. I nipped her neck again and squeezed her nipple harder.

I expected her to moan or sigh or make some kind of noise, but her jaw was clenched, and I noticed her hands gripping the ledge of the pool so hard her joints were white. I stopped moving and straightened.

After a moment, she turned her head. "What's wrong?"

"Why don't you tell me?" I no longer touched her, and she'd crossed one arm across both breasts, as if I hadn't just had my hands all over her and my cock about to split her.

She didn't meet my eyes, and her cheeks flamed pink. "Nothing's wrong. I thought you wanted to...?"

"Fuck you?" I finished the sentence for her, watching her flinch at the words. "Oh, I do, Raisa, but not like this."

She looked around at the blood-red water. "Not in the bath?"

I hoisted myself out of the water and stood over her beside the sunken pool, letting the water stream off me onto the stone floor. My cock was still hard and jutting out from my body. Her eyes darted to it, then quickly away.

"*Vaes*," I said, motioning with one hand for her to join me.

She was tentative as she got out, but I ignored her hesitation and her flushed cheeks. Grabbing her hand, I pulled her to the wall with nozzles and buttons, positioning her before I pressed a flat, square button. Hot air burst up from below, causing her to yelp and the water droplets on our skin to fly off or evaporate.

When we were both dry, I scooped the sheet off the floor. "You can wrap this around yourself."

She did, but she kept her head down as I led her out of the bathing chamber.

"You prefer the bed," she said as we crossed the room.

I dropped my grip on her wrist and turned abruptly. "I prefer a female who welcomes my touch."

To my surprise, she snapped her head up and met my gaze. "That wasn't part of the deal."

"Then we will make a new deal," I said, shocking myself with my own words. Why did I care so much that this female want me? I'd fucked plenty of females on pleasure planets who did not care one way or the other about me. It had never bothered me before. But this was different. She was different.

She narrowed her eyes at me. "What kind of new deal?"

"You are already mine." I ran a finger down the length of her neck to where her breasts swelled above the sheet. "You belong to me, but I do not want only your body. I want all of you, Raisa."

She blinked quickly. "I don't understand."

I leaned close to her. "I will have you, but only when you beg me for it."

"I will never beg you." But even as she said it, her pupils

dilated, and I could see through the sheet that her nipples were tight points.

"We will see." I crossed to where I'd dropped my kilt on the floor, stepping into it and fastening the belt around my waist. I left the armor hanging on the stand, but hooked my battle axe onto my belt.

"So that's it? I don't have to do anything anymore?"

I tried not to let the relief in her voice bother me, reminding myself that she did not know me, and she did not understand me or the Vandar yet.

I left my boots as I walked over to her, looping an arm around her back and jerking her tight to me. My tail wrapped around her body, keeping her from leaning away from me. "I did not say that. I said I would not fuck you until you tell me to. I did not say all the things I plan to do to you to make you beg for my cock. And believe me, little human, you will be begging for me to fuck you."

Her plump lips parted, and she sucked in a sharp breath. The sight of those curved lips made me think of the fullness of her ass cheeks and the soft folds I'd been stroking. I might want her to come to me willingly, but I was not above stealing a kiss from a female who belonged to me.

Tangling my free hand in her hair, I tilted her head back and crushed my mouth to hers. She struggled in my arms for a moment before moaning and lifting her arms to my shoulders. Fire ignited in my core and my cock ached, as I parted her lips with my tongue, taking possession of her mouth as I kissed her so deeply I wasn't sure where I ended, and she began.

Without breaking the kiss, I lifted her feet off the floor and walked her back to the bed, falling on it with her under me. The sheet slipped away between us as our bodies writhed, and she was naked beneath me, making soft noises as her tongue swirled with mine.

I tore myself away, panting as I looked down at her. "Tell me, Raisa."

The desire in her eyes was clear, but she only drew in shaky breaths as she looked up at me.

"Tell me you want me to fuck you," I said, my voice insistent.

Her body heaved underneath mine, and she'd hooked one leg around my waist, but still she did not speak. The wanting in her eyes had faded and there was only fear.

I jerked away from her, pressing my hard cock down with one hand as I turned and stormed out of the room, not giving a backward glance at the naked female on my bed. The naked female I'd brought on board as my prisoner for the express purpose of warming by bed and sucking my cock.

"*Tvek*," I growled as I pounded down the corridor in my bare feet. What was I doing making promises and deals with her? She was mine to do with as I pleased. I was a Raas of the Vandar. We took whatever we wanted, killed whomever we wanted, and fucked any female we desired. We did not let females hold power over us. Especially not human ones who should have been executed.

Why did it matter so much to me that this female want me? Why did I need her desire to be real? What was it about her that made me need to possess her soul as well as her body?

I passed a pair of warriors who clicked their heels when they saw me. I grunted acknowledgment but did not slow. I needed release and I needed counsel, and there was only one place I could get both.

I wound my way down a long staircase until I reached the

iron cage. I pressed my hands to the cool metal of the rungs before touching the communication panel to one side of the hinged door.

"Bron," my *majak* identified himself when he responded.

"It is Kratos," I told him. "Meet me in the battle ring."

CHAPTER

ELEVEN

Kratos

I lunged, swinging my bastard axe in a wide arc that sliced the air next to my *majak's* shoulder. Bron spun and brought his own sparring axe down hard, crashing against the steel of mine as I raised it to block his attack.

"I am glad we do not practice with real blades today, Raas." He grimaced as we held our weapons locked against each other. "I might leave with one less ear."

I stepped back and let my axe swing by my side as I sucked in a breath, the air hot in my lungs. We'd been fighting for a while and we both shone with sweat, our tails sagging near the floor. My muscles ached from the exertion, but at least my mind wasn't roiling.

"Rest," I commanded, striding over to one of the metal canisters hooked to the steel cage. Water beaded the sides, making it slippery to hold as I tipped it back and poured the cold water down my throat.

"Thank you, Raas." Bron crossed to his side of the battle ring and drank eagerly, as well.

I leaned over and let my arms dangle and the blood rush to my head. At least all my blood was no longer rushing to my cock. I stood and drew in another deep breath, trying to push all thoughts of the female from my mind.

Bron joined me, leaning his back against the high side of the circular cage. He was not as tall as me but his arms were even thicker, and he'd pulled his black hair up into a topknot. "We have not battled in a long time, Raas."

I grunted. "Too long. We were out of practice."

Bron grinned and swept a loose lock of hair off his forehead. "The Raas should speak for himself."

I leveled my gaze at him for a moment, then barked out a laugh. "You are the only warrior I would permit to say such a thing."

My *majak* returned my smile. "I know."

Although we were not related by blood, Bron was closer to me than even my own kin. We had started as raider apprentices on my father's warbird at the same time and had fought side by side since we were boys. Bron was the only Vandar on my crew who also knew what it was like to serve under my father and who knew how hard my father had driven me. He was the only one who understood why I had to be ruthless and brutal when I took over command. No one but Bron knew that my father's shadow hung over me still.

I swiped a hand across my slick brow. "Tell me what my crew thinks."

"Thinks, Raas?" Bron shifted from one foot to the other.

"You know what I mean, *majak*," I said, with a warning note in my voice. "What do they say about the Raas bringing a prisoner on board—a female?"

His gaze slid down for a moment. "Your crew is loyal, Raas. You know that."

I did not respond, waiting for him to tell me the truth. He was my most loyal friend, but he was also part of the crew. For the warriors to trust him, he could not be seen as one who would betray them. Even to me.

"They were surprised that you took her," he finally said. "You have never taken a captive or let a ship go."

"Do they think me weak for not killing the female captain?"

His head jerked up. "Not weak, Raas. Never weak." His mouth twitched. "They think the female you took must have a magic cunt. None would deny you that."

I choked out a laugh. "If it is magic, I would not know."

Silence hung thick between us before Bron spoke again. "So, that is why we are here."

I growled and rubbed a hand over the knot of muscles at the back of my neck. "I have spent my life being hunted. Anything I have, I have had to take by force and violence. But I cannot take what I need from her. I do not want her that way."

Bron cocked his head at me. "How do you want her, Raas?"

"I want her to give herself to me not because she has to but because she wants to." I punched one fist into my open palm. "For once, I want to possess something that has not been taken."

"Kratos." Bron put a hand on my arm. He was one of the very few who addressed me by my given name, and only rarely, but it felt good to hear the familiarity of it, instead of the title I heard from the rest of the crew. "Do not concern yourself with this. She will come around. You are Raas. Any female would be lucky to share your bed."

"I do not want just any female," I said, knowing I sounded like a petulant child.

Bron let out a breath and dropped his voice. "Soon we will be at Jaldon. There, you will have your pick of beautiful, willing females." He nudged me. "You remember the twins from Felaris? Certainly, they can take your mind off this human?"

I thought back to the three-breasted, alien females with pale-pink skin who worked as a team to pleasure males. I'd spent many a night at the pleasure house with them, and always left spent and satisfied. But even the thought of having my cock sucked by two eager mouths did not banish Astrid from my mind.

"We will see," I said. "At least the Zagrath will not follow us to Jaldon."

"They do not venture to the dark part of the sector." He nudged me. "Too many Vandar raider hordes."

I allowed myself a sigh. The crew needed a break even more than I did. It would be good for our horde of ships to set down on Jaldon. And it was always good for a pleasure planet when a Vandar horde arrived. Vandar never took from those who did not support the empire. And pleasure planets operating on the dark outskirts of the sector wanted nothing to do with the imperial forces. We might liberate goods from the Zagrath, but we always paid handsomely for our drinking and whoring.

"It will be good to be back on Jaldon," I admitted. Good to stop chasing.

"We will arrive soon."

Bron and I both turned to see Corvak standing outside the ring. He had approached without either of us hearing, no mean feat on a cavernous ship that seemed to echo every footstep.

"Excellent," I said, making my voice boom. "Any threats on long range sensors?"

"Negative." Corvak watched as Bron and I descended the steps leading to the battle ring. "No Zagrath near Jaldon or anywhere close to our route."

I gave him a curt nod. "Will I see you at your usual pleasure house, cousin?"

His eyebrows lifted. "You intend to partake?"

I clapped a hand on his back, harder than I usually would. "Don't I always?"

He flinched slightly. "I thought that with your prisoner—"

"You thought wrong." I cut him off before he could finish his sentence. "Just because I took the female for my pleasure does not mean I cannot enjoy the company of others. I am still Raas, am I not?"

"Of course," Corvak said quickly, his eyes darting to Bron and then back to me. "I would never suggest that you aren't—"

"I know you wouldn't," I said. "You have watched me slaughter enough to know that my hunger is not easily satisfied—for killing or for fucking."

He inclined his head to me. "I am glad to hear it, Raas. There are many Zagrath left to kill."

"But not today," I said to my battle chief. "Today is our reward for helping to purge the galaxy of the controlling hand of the empire."

I hooked my sparring axe on the outside of the ring and

took long strides up the stairs, my officers falling in step behind me. I hoped that between burning off some energy with Bron, and burning off some with the Felaris twins, I could shake the desire for Astrid that threatened to consume me.

TWELVE

Astrid

When he returned, I was dressed and sitting at one side of the gleaming black dining table near the glass overlooking space.

He seemed momentarily startled, but his eyes lit on the dishes spread out in front of me, the rich scents wafting up. "They brought food. Good. I am starving."

So, he wasn't going to talk about the way he'd left. I guessed Vandar warlords didn't like to rehash arguments or discuss their feelings. Fine by me. I definitely didn't want to talk about how breathless he'd made me. Or how I'd been moments away from begging him to fuck me, even if I wouldn't have been able to say the word.

"And clothes," I said, gesturing to the dress I wore.

His gaze traveled to the loose, blue fabric that spilled

down from ties at my shoulders. There was little shape to it, and it pooled at my feet when I stood. If this was how Vandar women dressed, no wonder he'd thought my snug pants and T-shirt were obscene.

The Raas cleared his throat, looking away from me as he took off his armor and hung it up. "It looks good on you, although I would not have minded if you'd continued to wear that sheet—or nothing at all."

My face warmed, but I didn't reply. His body glistened with sweat as he walked across the room toward me, and I wondered where he'd been. Not that I was going to ask. Just looking at his bulging muscles flushed from exertion made my throat tighten and heat throb between my legs.

"You should have eaten," he said, taking the bench across from me. "You must be hungry."

I didn't tell him that I'd nibbled some of the dishes, but wasn't sure what the Vandar concoctions were. There was also no silverware. The attendant who'd brought the clothes and food hadn't been all that helpful, either. He'd seemed bothered by my presence, and shocked that I didn't know the dishes he'd placed on the table. The only thing I'd been able to get out of him was that the ship would be stopping soon. On a pleasure planet, no less. He'd seemed pleased to share that with me.

I watched as Kratos poured some lumpy, orange stew into a bowl, tore off some flat bread, and began using the bread to scoop mouthfuls into his mouth. I tentatively followed suit, tearing off bits of bread and attempting to use them like a spoon.

No problem, I thought. *I can eat like this. How hard can it be?*

After my piece of bread broke off and I'd dropped a blob of food onto my chest for the second time, I heard a stifled guffaw from across the table. Looking up sharply, I saw that Kratos was trying to hide his laughter behind his hand.

Heat rushed to my cheeks, and I threw down my bread. "This isn't that easy, you know!"

He stopped laughing. "I am sorry. I had no idea you didn't know how to eat."

"I know how to eat," I snapped at him. "I just don't know how to eat without a fork or a spoon. This bread keeps falling apart."

He pushed back his chair and stood, walking quickly to my side of the table and sitting on the bench next to me. He plucked a flat round of bread from a bowl and held it up. "You need to use this to wrap the food, but you must fold it first."

I watched carefully as he bent the bread back on itself, making a double layer. Then he used it to pick up a piece of shredded meat and pop it into his mouth. As he chewed, he gestured for me to try.

I parroted his movements, folding the bread and then trying to grab a bite of food, but the morsel slipped out and splattered onto the table. I looked up at him, but he'd already wiped the smile off his face.

Standing, he came around behind me, wrapping his arms around my body and lifting my hands in his.

"You don't have to feed me," I said, indignant and slightly embarrassed that I couldn't manage to eat without making a mess.

"I'm not feeding you." He put his head next to mine and his deep voice sent a shiver skating down my spine. "I'm teaching you."

I swallowed hard, my heart fluttering like a bird desperately trying to escape a cage. Having him so close made fear and desire battle within me, a feeling I was not used to.

Cupping my hands in his much larger ones, Kratos guided me to pick up the bread. "You cannot hold it too hard, or it will tear."

I nodded, but my body shook as he moved my hand so that I picked up a bit of food from a platter. His grip on me was gentle as he guided the food to my mouth, his finger brushing my lower lip.

I closed my mouth and chewed, the meat warm and savory on my tongue. He had not let go of my hands, and I could feel his eyes on me.

"Do you like it?" he asked.

For a brief moment, I wasn't sure if he meant the food or him holding me. I turned to meet his gaze, his face so close to mine that his breath was warm on my cheek. His eyes were black, and a vein thrummed in the side of his neck. If I had been standing, my knees would have given way.

"It's delicious," I finally managed to whisper.

"You seem surprised."

"I've never eaten Vandar food before."

His gaze held mine. "That is not why."

"I didn't know a Raas of the Vandar could be gentle," I said before I could think better of it.

He nodded, his eyes drifting to my lips. "You make me want to be gentle." He dropped my hands and captured my jaw in one palm. "You also make me want to tear the clothes off your body and fuck you right here on this table."

I inhaled a shallow breath, my mouth going dry.

"But I will not do that, Raisa," he whispered, dragging his thumb across my bottom lip. "I do not want you that way. Not the first time, at least."

When he kissed me, it was so soft that I barely felt his lips against mine. I raised a hand to his face and leaned in, wanting more of him. He responded instantly, his lips moving against mine and his tongue delving into my mouth. I moaned when he threaded his fingers in my hair and tilted my head back to taste more of me.

When he pulled away, he rested his forehead against mine, his breaths labored. "It is hard to control myself with you." He stood and looked down at me. "But I should stop kissing you, if you are not ready to tell me what I want to hear."

I didn't say anything, even though part of me wanted nothing more than what he did as well.

He jerked his gaze away from me and returned to his side of the table in a few long strides. "You will beg me soon enough. I will wait."

I wanted to tell him that he was going to be waiting for a long time, but I wasn't sure that was true anymore. I couldn't deny that there was something about this brutal warlord that was the opposite of anything I'd expected, or anything I'd been told about the Vandar. Something that pulled me to him and made me want to know more.

I stared down at my food, my lips still buzzing from his touch. "I hear we're stopping soon."

"You heard?" The softness had left his voice. "Where are you hearing things, Raisa?"

I lifted my head and saw him glaring across the table at me. "It's not like I'm hanging out with your Vandar buddies on the bridge. The guy who brought the food mentioned it."

His expression relaxed, and he resumed eating. "We are stopping. The crew needs some release."

"At a pleasure planet, right?" I asked, watching his face to see if he'd lie to me. Since I'd been a child, I been able to read people's expressions and know if they were lying.

He glanced up and met my gaze. "Yes. We are stopping on

the pleasure planet, Jaldon." His mouth twitched. "Do you have a problem with that?"

I shrugged. "Why would I care what your crew does? Or who they do?"

"I am glad." He stood, taking a long swig of wine from his goblet and wiping his hand across his mouth. "I will return tomorrow, but if you need anything you can press the panel to the side of the door and an attendant will bring you whatever you require."

"Wait, you're going to be getting off at the pleasure planet?" My voice sounded much shriller than I'd intended it to.

He crossed his arms over his chest. "You have no problem with my crew blowing off steam with women and whiskey, yet you would deny me the same release?"

I stood to face him, not sure why I had the urge to slap the smug look off his face. "Do whatever you want to do. I don't care." I spun on my heel and stalked away from him.

Before I'd gotten a few steps, he'd come up behind me and snaked one arm tightly around my waist, pulling me hard against him. "I think you do care, Raisa. I think you want me as much as I want you."

I shook my head, even as I felt my nipples harden and my pulse race.

He stroked the back of his hand down my face even as his tail dipped underneath my skirt and stroked up the front of my leg. "Just tell me what I want to hear, and I'll stay here with you, instead."

As much as my body ached for him and as good as his tail felt between my thighs, I could not submit to the Vandar warlord so easily. I could not be so weak. My sister would never have given in so easily. I shook my head again, and he roared, pushing away from me.

"If this is what you want, Raisa," he rasped.

I turned and watched him back away from me, his expression both menacing and tortured.

He growled once more before turning his back on me. "It is done."

When he'd stomped out of the room, I stumbled to the bed, my body shaking as I sank down on it.

THIRTEEN

Kratos

"Which one pleases you, Raas?" The alien madam swept a green arm wide as she simpered at me.

The females stood in a row for me to inspect, and behind me, some of my warriors shuffled in anticipation for their turn. Although the warriors from all the ships in my horde had scattered throughout the city, the pleasure house I had chosen contained the most beautiful and exotic females. It was the house my command deck warriors frequented and where I had spent many a pleasurable night.

I cast my gaze down the line of scantily clad pleasurers— tall Grexians with double-jointed pelvises, curvy Borans who were so top-heavy they looked like they would tip over, and blue-skinned Haralli with wings—but none of them made my pulse quicken.

I was still fuming from Astrid's latest refusal and having serious doubts about the promise I'd made her. What was the point of being a Raas of the Vandar if I could not take what I wanted—anything I wanted?

"That one," I finally said, pointing to a willowy Teraxian with black hair. At least she would not remind me of the small, light-haired human back in my quarters.

The creature moved toward me, her hips swaying as she walked. She hooked her arm through mine, giving me a practiced sultry smile. "The Raas honors me with his attention."

I didn't respond. I had only come to the pleasure house because it was what my crew expected, and what I'd promised both Bron and Corvak. It would prove to them all that the female I'd taken as my captive did not hold sway over me. I was still the Raas, who could outdrink and outfuck any of them.

I let my eyes wander as the Teraxian led me up the sweeping staircase. The house was only three levels, with rooms circling the soaring entrance hall and balconies extending into the center. The lights were turned low—to appeal to our sensitive Vandar eyes—with illuminated filaments crisscrossing the empty space between the balconies and creating a glowing web of light.

I glanced down as we continued to the top level of the house and saw some of my crew gathered around tables on the first level, as topless females walked through the room passing out shots of bitter Jaldon whiskey. I saw Corvak pull one serving girl down onto his lap roughly and squeeze one of her three breasts. She wiggled in his grasp but did not get up. The Vandar paid well for having free run of the premises and of the females inside it.

"Right in here, Raas." The alien female waved me into a room that was fully equipped for pleasure. Aside from the huge bed, there was a mirror on the ceiling, a swing hanging in another corner, and a selection of whips and restraints displayed on the wall.

She closed the door and led me to the long, padded bench at the foot of the bed. "How should I pleasure you first, Raas?" she purred as she began unhooking my belt.

I was silent as she removed both my belt and kilt, running a hand down the length of my tail. My body jerked slightly as she reached the tip, swirled her fingers around it, and squeezed. It was clear that this female knew what to do with Vandar tails.

When she saw my cock, she made the noises of appreciation I would have expected from her. She was good, I would give her that. If I had not been to as many pleasure houses as I had, I might have believed her moans. But they were not real.

Not like the sounds Astrid had made when I'd kissed her. I'd felt the human's genuine desire coupled with her fear, and it had been intoxicating.

The Teraxian pushed me down on the bench and knelt between my legs, fisting my cock and eyeing it with well-practiced desire. I closed my eyes and leaned back, trying to convince myself that it was Astrid who was sucking me, and not this well-seasoned pleasurer. I imagined that it was my little human's mouth taking all of me as she played with my tail and making hungry noises while she did. I fisted my hand in her hair and moved her head up and down, thrusting my cock down her throat. But as much as I tried to imagine Astrid, I knew it was not her.

I opened my eyes and sat up so quickly the Teraxian flew back, yelping in surprise, a look of irritation crossing her face as she dropped my tail. She quickly resumed smiling at me, dabbing at the corners of her mouth. When I stood and pulled up my kilt, her smile faltered once more. "Is Raas displeased? Would he prefer to tie me up? Or perhaps whip me with his tail?"

I fastened my belt and shook my head. "I am not displeased with you. I am merely distracted. I will pay your madam for a full night with you. Why don't you take the night off and get some rest?"

She sauntered toward me, splaying her hands across my chest. "I'd rather have a big, strong Raas fuck me."

I grasped her wrists. "It will not be this one, female. Not tonight."

She sighed, her voice losing its seductive lilt. "Fine, but don't tell Kyrva I didn't try." Her eyes dropped down. "And I should get extra for deep-throating *that*."

I almost laughed, preferring this honest version of the female more than her sexy persona. "I will give you extra for *that*."

I left her standing with her hands on her hips, closing the door behind me and almost bumping into Bron in the corridor.

He eyed me then the door. "You are usually not done with one so quickly, Kratos. Was she no good?"

"She was fine," I said. I saw that he was not with a female. "Where is yours?"

He nodded his head at a spot down the hall where two identical females were walking. They paused, looked back over their shoulders and beckoned him with their fingers and matching giggles.

"Twins from Felaris," I said, grinning at my *majak*.

He shrugged. "It has been a long time. But if you would prefer—"

I waved a hand at him. "No, my friend. You enjoy them. I was just heading downstairs to have a drink."

"You are sure?"

I pounded a hand on his back. "When you are done, come join me for some Jaldon whiskey."

I left him and walked purposefully down the stairs, the loud music and laughter getting louder as I reached the first floor. I paused at the bottom of the stairs to let a blue-skinned female flit by me, one of my warriors chasing her in what appeared to be a game of strip tag. Crossing to a table, I straddled a bench next to my battle chief.

"What happened to the pretty serving girl?" I asked, nudging him.

He peered at me over a large iron tankard. "Too busy."

I flicked my eyes up. "You don't wish to take a room?"

He lifted his drink. "I wanted to unwind with a few Parnolian ales, first."

I waved a hand at a server, pointing to Corvak's large ale to indicate I wanted the same. "A good choice."

"And you?" Corvak asked, one of his dark eyebrows lifting. "What happened with your pleasurer?"

I thought back to the striking Teraxian. "She was very efficient."

Corvak snorted a laugh. "You're sure that is it?"

I picked up the ale that was placed in front of me and took a swig of the cold, frothy drink. "I'm sure. Why? You do not wish to drink with your Raas?"

He straightened. "That is not what I meant. But you usually spend much more time upstairs than down."

I twitched one shoulder. "Maybe it has been too long

since I drank with my warriors." I lifted my ale and my voice. "To Lokken!"

All the warriors around me lifted their own tankards and glasses to the ancient god. "To Lokken!"

We all drank and then thudded our drinks onto the table. There were more roars and cheers, and one of the warriors yelled, "To the Raas!"

I nodded as my crew bellowed their approval, chanting "Raas" over and over until I stood, holding my hands up. I lifted my ale in salute and chugged the remains in a single, long gulp, pounding the metal tankard on the table.

"Another round for the Vandar warriors," I called over the raucous shouting, and servers scurried out from behind the bar carrying full trays. A new tankard was placed in front of me, the golden contents sloshing over the sides.

When I sat back down, Corvak eyed me, nodding. "It has been a while since you have done this."

"It is like in the beginning, no?" I asked, remembering the days when I was a new Raas, and I would drink with my warriors almost every night.

"I'd thought maybe you were here because you did not want to take a female tonight. Because of the female in your quarters."

I shook my head. "I told you she holds no sway over me. She is my prisoner."

"So, you do not feel loyalty to her?"

I laughed, even as my stomach tightened. "No more loyalty than I would to one of these creatures." I motioned to a winged Haralli who fluttered overhead.

"I am glad to hear it." Corvak raised his glass to me and drank.

I also took a drink, although my gut churned at the lie. I did not lie to my crew, and I had never felt the need to hide anything from my battle chief before. So why was I compelled to hide my feelings for the human? Why did the small female affect me so much?

I'd just wiped the back of my hand across my mouth when I saw the young Vandar apprentice pushing his way through the crowd. His eyes were wide, and his chest was heaving as if he'd run a long distance.

"Raas!" He said when he spotted me. "*Vaes!*"

Corvak stood quickly, knocking his chair over behind him.

My heart plummeted to my stomach. "Is it As—"

"It's the Zagrath," he said, his words a fast jumble. "They found us. They're boarding our ships."

I was already running for the door before he finished his sentence. Astrid. They were trying to take Astrid.

FOURTEEN

Astrid

I could not believe that he'd walked out on me to go to some alien whorehouse. I stopped pacing long enough to stamp my foot hard.

"Infuriating alien," I muttered to myself. "Just who the hell does he think he is?" I slapped a hand over my mouth then dropped it. If I was going to live among the Vandar and with a warlord who irritated me so much, I should probably get comfortable with cursing. "The big jerk."

Okay, baby steps.

Obviously, he thought he was the warlord of a powerful horde of violent Vandar raiders who could take whatever they wanted. And, technically, he was right. He'd taken me hadn't he?

I was a citizen of the empire, and he'd captured me like I was his for the taking. My face warmed as I thought about his big, rough hands on me. He clearly thought he could do with me what he pleased.

"Well, think again, asshole." I smiled at myself. This swearing thing wasn't so bad. Then I frowned again thinking of Kratos.

I tried not to dwell on how my body had responded to his touch or how I'd almost begged him to fuck me. My face flushed even thinking the word.

A momentary lapse, I told myself. As gorgeous as he was, I could not let myself fall for him. Even though a part of me wanted to know what it would be like to surrender to someone as big and powerful as him.

"No way can the first guy you sleep with be a warlord of the Vandar, Astrid," I whispered, as I sank onto the foot of the bed. It was absurd, although everything about the situation was ridiculous.

I still didn't understand why he'd taken a prisoner when the Vandar didn't do that. Why had he brought a woman on board when it was obviously not done? And why me, of all people? There was nothing special about me.

If he'd taken my sister, I would have understood. Tara was beautiful and strong, and a fitting match for a Vandar. But me? I shook my head. None of this made any sense.

Before I could slip down the familiar rabbit hole of self-doubt, I heard the sound of blaster fire outside the door. I stood quickly. That wasn't right. The ship had landed, along with the rest of the horde of Vandar spaceships, and as far as I knew, the crews were busy whoring and drinking. Raas had said there would be some warriors left on board in case I needed anything, but I couldn't imagine why they'd be firing weapons.

Loud shouts and the pounding of heavy footsteps made my eyes dart around the room. Was the ship being attacked?

I knew there were plenty of aliens who would love the chance to turn the Vandar over to the Zagrath, and taking a Vandar horde would be a particularly impressive haul. But Raas Kratos had seemed confidant they were landing on a safe planet. Not only that, but the Vandar flew using their invisibility shielding, so it would have been impossible to follow them. So, who was firing outside in the corridors?

The dim lighting flickered and then went out, plunging me into total darkness. The panel by the door also went dark, which meant I couldn't call for help.

"Just great," I said under my breath.

More sounds of blasters and screaming came from the other side of the door, then there was silence. I held my breath, waiting for more noise, but there was nothing. Had the attackers gone? Had the Vandar fought them off?

After a few minutes, I smelled the distinct scent of smoke drifting underneath my door. Was the ship on fire? Panic clawed at my throat. Who knew I was in here? Was anyone still alive to get me out, or had all the Vandar been killed and the attackers gone? If they'd decided to burn the ship instead of capture it, I was as good as dead.

I gathered my voluminous dress in one hand and made my way forward, extending my other arm so I wouldn't walk into a wall. When I'd reached the other side of the room, I groped until I found the door.

"Here goes nothing," I said to myself as I pressed both hands against the seam of the door and pulled back as hard as I could. To my surprise, it began to open. The loss of power must have disengaged the locking mechanism.

I pulled until I'd made a space wide enough to fit through, and I eased myself out of the room. When I was in the corridor, I saw faint emergency lights glowing on the floor, so I started to follow them away from the smell of smoke.

Taking careful steps, I made my way down one staircase, pausing when I heard the echoing of footsteps approaching. I didn't know if they were Vandar or attackers, so I ducked down a darkened hallway, holding my breath as the sound got closer.

"The Raas' quarters must be here somewhere," a gravelly voice said, as the group stopped not far from me.

"If we hadn't disengaged the power, maybe we could have found them faster," another voice said.

"We had to do that to stop the fire," someone else snapped.

"Who thought it would be a great idea to shoot the electrical systems to start the fire?"

A loud grunt. "Enough! We don't have time to stand around arguing. We have to find the female before the Vandar realize we're here and return to the ship. If we haven't gotten her by then, we're as good as dead."

My pulse quickened. These attackers were here to find me? Had my sister sent a crew of rescuers after me? Or had she alerted the Zagrath Empire that one of her crew was illegally taken and they'd sent a crew? Either way, I was rescued. I let out a long breath, preparing to step out and reveal myself.

"So, do we take her or kill her?" the first voice asked.

I froze. Kill me?

"We take her, and then dispose of her. We can't leave the body here. Those were the orders."

"Then let's go," one of the aliens sighed. "I want to get this job done and get the hell off this ship."

They ran off, passing me huddled in the dark with one hand pressed tightly over my mouth so I wouldn't scream. Why were these attackers here to kill me? It made no sense. If they knew about me at all, why wouldn't they be here to rescue me? Unless they wanted to take me and kill me to strike a blow against the Raas directly. But who of his enemies knew he'd taken me?

I realized that my entire body was shaking as I stood in the dark. I tried to suck in deep lungfuls of air to calm myself, but knowing that a bunch of people were on the ship for the express purpose of finding me and killing me made it hard to breathe.

For a brief moment, I wished Kratos was with me. He wouldn't let anyone hurt me, and I had a pretty good feeling that whoever these alien attackers were, they wouldn't stand a chance against him or his Vandar warriors. The only reason the attackers had been able to take the ship was because the Raas and his crew had left it.

Where are you, Kratos?

I would have given anything to see the huge warlord, even though I'd been angry enough to kill him not so long ago.

More footsteps echoed, and I pressed myself against the wall, glad I was as petite as I was. At least it was dark, and I was small. They would have a hard time finding me in a ship so cavernous. All I had to do was stay hidden until the Vandar returned to the ship.

Suddenly, the lights within the ship turned back on. Even though it was still pretty dim, as was standard for the Vandar, I was no longer hidden.

"You have got to be freaking kidding me," I muttered to myself, glancing around the empty hallway.

I needed to find a place to hide, and a hallway wasn't it. Peeking around the corner and seeing that no one was coming, I made a dash for it. I ran on my tiptoes, holding my ridiculously full skirts up to keep from tripping.

I rounded a corner and saw a wide hallway lined with

steel barrels and stacked tall with boxes. From the other end, I saw the red glow of blaster fire and heard a cacophony of yells. Someone was coming. I didn't know if it was the Vandar, or the aliens trying to kill me.

I was out of time, and out of great options. Eyeing the row of barrels, I noticed a narrow space behind them and the wall. Sucking in my belly so much that it hurt, I wedged myself behind the steel barrels, crouching down so my head wouldn't poke over the top.

The battle was getting closer to me. My heart hammered in my chest as aliens ran by me. Even though it was almost deafening as the steel floors rattled and blasters fired, I held my breath for fear that one of them would somehow hear me. When I was sure they'd all gone, I released a breath.

They'd gone. They hadn't seen me.

Then a hand closed over my wrist.

CHAPTER
FIFTEEN

Kratos

I ran through the narrow alleyways of the city toward the shipyard. My crew ran behind me, our pounding boots making the ground tremble and causing windows in the towering buildings to slam shut as we passed.

We'd left the pleasure house in a matter of moments, the rooms emptying out as the battle cry was raised and warriors tugging on kilts as they'd thundered down the stairs. I hadn't waited for anyone, drawing my battle axe and leading the way through the Jaldon city.

"How did this happen?" I called over my shoulder to Corvak, who was close at my heels.

"The boy said a small war party killed the guards and boarded the lead ship."

"Not the others?"

"I do not think so, but I did not take much time to question him, Raas."

I nodded and focused my eyes forward as the stone pillars fronting the shipyard came into view—along with a plume of black smoke rising from my ship.

"*Tvek!*" I growled, when I saw the dark column curling into the air.

Angry murmurs rose up behind me like a swarm of fury. We barreled through the gates and made short work of the hardpacked ground between us and my ship.

I didn't pause when we reached the wide ramp, but I raised my battle axe as we rushed up it. "Find the attackers. Kill them all!"

My crew raced through the ship, ducking down corridors and up staircases in search of the invaders. I had one destination. I had to reach my quarters and make sure Astrid was unhurt.

My heart skittered in my chest as I reached the door and saw that it had been forced open. Bile rose up in my throat, but I forced it down. The Zagrath had no reason to harm Astrid. If anything, they had probably been sent to take her back. For a moment, I regretted leaving her sister and the crew of the pathetic freighter alive. If I hadn't been merciful, this would not have happened.

I pushed the door open wider, rushing in and hearing a click behind me. I pivoted and dodged to one side, barely missing the blaster fire that warmed the tip of my ear. With a roar, I swung my axe and the soldier stumbled back. He clearly wasn't used to hand-to-hand combat, and he fired again, even more wildly than the first time. The blaster missed me, but hit my headboard, searing a hole through one of the iron shields welded together.

"That shield was over a thousand rotations old," I growled, turning back to the soldier.

His expression was terrified. I noticed that he didn't wear the uniform of a Zagrath imperial fighter. Instead, his clothes were worn, and his blaster outdated. He had heavy ridges over his eyes and his skin was jaundiced. A Lussite. The race was known for being thugs, but not very good ones. I had never heard of Lussites daring to attack a Vandar horde before.

I swung my axe again and knocked the blaster out of his hand, taking the tip of one finger with it. He screamed and clutched his hand as blood spurted from it.

"Why are you here?" I raised my axe high, waiting for his answer.

The soldier looked up, his face twisted in agony. "For the girl. We're here for the girl."

I'd been right. They had been after Astrid. But they weren't Zagrath. Not that the empire hadn't been known to hire out for its less important missions.

"How did you find us?" I asked, hearing the shake in my voice.

"We were told the Vandar horde that took the human would show up at Jaldon, so we waited."

"Told?" I watched him cradle his hand and eye the blaster on the floor across the room. "Who told you?"

He shook his head hard. "I don't know. I don't make the plans. I just do what I'm told and get paid."

So, mercenaries. My eyes went to his clothing again. Not very well-paid ones. I almost felt bad for killing this foot soldier.

He used my hesitation to dive across the floor for his blaster. Without thinking twice, I brought my axe down across his neck. I did not feel bad enough about killing him to die for it.

I was heaving when I spun around and took in the rest of the room. He clearly hadn't found Astrid. Where was she?

My quarters were spartan, and my furniture stark. There were very few places to hide. I strode into the bathing chamber, plunging my arm into the green water and then into the red, the only pools opaque enough to hide in. Nothing. My gaze quickly scanned the rest of the stone room, but the long counter and open shower did not provide any secret nooks.

As I walked out of the bathing chamber, Bron ran into my quarters. His face was flushed and his hair sweaty. He glanced down at the body and the growing pool of blood on the shiny, black floor. "Where is the girl?"

"Gone," I said, the word like bile on my tongue. "She escaped from my quarters."

"She could have been running from them," he said, pointing his axe at the dead fighter.

"They were here to take her back."

A look of understanding crossed his face. "This was not an attack on the Vandar?"

I gave a single hard shake of my head. "This was a rescue attempt." I readjusted my grip on my axe. "One we must ensure is not successful."

"Yes, Raas," Bron said. "We will find her. I will tell the warriors."

"She is not to be harmed," I said, as he backed out of my doorway. "If she needs to be punished, I will be the one to do so."

I gave a final look at the dead Lussite on my floor as I stormed after my *majak*. If they had laid a hand on my female, they would all find themselves with one less head.

The ship was filled with the sound of battles, and I knew

that the screams were coming from the Lussite invaders as they were being hunted down by my crew. Soon the invaders would be eliminated, and we would send a clear message to anyone else who attempted to take what was mine.

I walked through the empty hallways, listening for soft footfall or a female's voice. She would not have been able to enter any of the other chambers without the proper code, so she was either with the Lussites, or she was hiding.

Winding my way through the ship, I followed two of my warriors as they battled a group of invaders. Even though the Lussites fought with blasters, my raiders were highly skilled with their axes, and soon there were more alien bodies littering our corridors. As my warriors ran off to find more of the enemy, I stepped over the bodies and paused.

Had I heard the last exhalation of death or something else? Turning slowly, I prodded at the bodies with my toe. No, they were truly dead. Then I peered over a collection of barrels waiting to be offloaded, and saw a flash of pale hair.

My breath caught in my throat. Even though the space was tight, she'd managed to squeeze herself behind the barrels. She was hiding, and she was shaking like a leaf.

I reached for her wrist to pull her up. She jerked away and attempted to back up, even though she was wedged tight.

"I'm not going with you," she cried. "Let go!"

I lifted her up and set her down in front of me. "You thought you could escape from me?"

She looked up at me, and her mouth gaped open.

Before she could say anything else I scooped her up and tossed her over one shoulder. "Don't you know by now that you are mine?"

"I wasn't running away from you," she said, bouncing as I

carried her back through the ship. "Well, at first I was, but then I wasn't."

"You thought you'd leave with the mercenaries sent to rescue you?" My blood boiled as I walked faster. "You thought you would leave me?"

"No." She hit my back with the flat of her hands. "Will you stop for a second? That's not what happened."

"I know they came for you." I climbed a staircase, her body jostling roughly against mine. In a few long steps, I'd reached my quarters.

"I wasn't trying to escape with them, Kratos," she said, slapping my back hard. "You're being crazy."

I swung her down once I'd passed through my doors and crossed to my bed, pushing her backwards so she fell back onto the dark sheets. I loomed over her and planted my hands on either side of her face. "If I'm crazy it's because you make me crazy."

Her eyes were wide. "I wasn't hiding from you. I was hiding from the guys trying to kill me."

"Who do you think was trying to kill you, Raisa?" I was breathing hard as I hovered over her, every muscle in my body tensed with both rage and desire.

"They were." She waved a hand toward the body on my floor.

I frowned at her. "You are not making sense, human. They were here to take you from me."

She pressed her lips together. "They were going to kill me. I heard them talking. They were paid to find me and take me off your ship and then kill me."

I stilled, the blood slowing as it coursed through my veins. "You are sure?"

"I heard them talking to each other. They didn't know I

was hiding nearby," she said. "If I'd wanted to leave you, why was I hiding on the ship? I could have just run off."

I studied her face and saw no deception in her eyes. Plus, her words made sense. It had not been a rescue attempt. Someone wanted my female dead.

Standing quickly, I dragged the dead Lussite from my quarters and dumped him in the corridor. When I returned, I closed the door and crossed to where she still lay on the bed, propped up on her elbows watching me.

"Thank you," she said, her voice trembling.

"You are welcome, Raisa." I leaned over her and stroked a hand down her cheek. "I will not let anyone hurt you. You are mine, and I will guard you with my life, as will every one of my warriors."

She drew in an uneven breath and nodded. "But someone doesn't want me to be yours."

I lowered my body until it was flush with hers—my hardness pressing against her softness—bracing myself with my elbows so I didn't crush her. "What do you want?"

CHAPTER
SIXTEEN

Astrid

I felt lost in his gaze as he stared down at me, his dark eyes flaring and molten. Surely, my heart was hammering hard enough for him to feel it in his own chest.

"What do you want, Raisa?" he repeated, his words soft but urgent.

I didn't know what I wanted, but as crazy as it was, I knew he felt right. He also felt incredibly huge and hard as his body covered mine, and I was reminded again just how much bigger he was than me—everywhere.

I cleared my throat. "What does Raisa mean?"

His eyes flickered for a moment. "You want to know what Raisa means?"

I nodded.

"My lady," he husked.

"Oh." I'd expected it to mean mate or concubine. I hadn't expected it to be so...nice.

"Are you?" He lowered his mouth to my throat and feathered a kiss across the skin where my pulse fluttered.

I opened my mouth to answer but my mouth went dry as his tongue trailed up my neck to my ear. The only sound that came out of my mouth was a breathy whimper.

"I'll take that as a yes," he murmured.

"You take everything as a yes."

He stopped, and I sucked in a breath. Had I made him angry by saying that?

Then his body began to shake with laughter. "You are right. I do take your fast breathing and flushed skin and wide eyes as a yes. Because you are shy with your words." He lifted his face, so it hovered above mine. "I know you want me, Raisa. I know you want this."

He was right. My body betrayed me every time he was near, but bells still sounded the alarm in the far recesses of my brain.

"But I don't know why you want *me*," I said. "You're the Raas and you're gorgeous and you can have any woman you want—and probably have. Why does it matter so much that you...?"

"Claim you as mine?" He brushed a strand of hair off my forehead, his gaze moving across my face. "You are so small, yet there is strength in you that should not be there. You should not be able to deny me, but you do. I do not want you, Astrid. I *need* you. There is no other female who has ever captivated me so. There is no one who has ever refused me before."

"But you still went to the whorehouse," I said, hating the childish tone of my voice. I didn't want to fight with him like I had earlier, but I couldn't let it go.

"Only to be with my crew and to reassure them that I am the same Raas they have always known."

"So, you weren't with a..." I hesitated over the word, "...pleasurer?"

"I selected one, but I could not bring myself to fuck her." His brows furrowed. "Does it upset you to think of me with another female?"

"Well, yeah." For a warlord, he could be a bit clueless. "If you're telling me I'm your Raisa, your lady or whatever, it's not cool to run off to alien whorehouses." My voice broke. "You left me all alone."

He cupped my chin in his hand. "I am sorry, Raisa. I didn't think you cared."

I hadn't thought I'd cared, either. I knew I *shouldn't* care a thing about the warlord who'd taken me away from everything I'd ever known. But for some inexplicable reason, I did. "I guess I do."

"Good," he rasped, as he crushed his mouth to mine.

I was startled by the intensity of his kiss, but I parted my lips and met his tongue with my own. Kratos took one of my hands and threaded his fingers with mine, lifting it over my head and pressing it down into the silky bed coverings. He did the same with my other hand until both hands were pinned over my head as he kissed me deeply. I tried to move my arms, but he held them tightly, grinding himself into me as I writhed beneath him.

"Raisa," he whispered when he broke the kiss, and I lay panting beneath him. Moving my hands so that he pinned both down with only one of his large hands, he slipped his free hand down to my thigh.

Even though his fingers were callused—no doubt from swinging his battle axe—his touch was soft as he slid his hand under my skirts, gathering them as he moved up the length of my thigh. He shifted his body, opening my legs with his knees. Then I felt the feathery tip of his tail stroking between them and my eyelids fluttered with desire. I never imagined a tail could be so sexy, but his soft strokes made me bite my lip to keep from moaning out loud.

When he removed his tail and settled his broad body between my legs, I felt the loss of his tail. That is, until I felt the hardness of his cock pressing against my inner thigh. Holy crap.

"You're wet for me," he said, the black pupils of his eyes so enlarged that there was only a hint of iris.

My cheeks warmed, embarrassment at my obvious arousal causing my face to flame.

"It is a good thing, my beautiful one. I like to feel your slickness. I would like to taste it even more."

I jerked at that. Taste it? I'd never imagined that such a battle-hardened Vandar raider would want to bury his face between my legs. "You don't have to."

"Have to?" His low chuckle sent tremors through my chest. "Remember, Raisa. I am Raas. I do not do anything I do not want to do, so if I say I want to lick your sweet, little cunt, it is because I want to."

Hearing him talk about me like that sent a jolt through me, and I shivered in anticipation. Even if I couldn't bring myself to say the words, I liked hearing them. And I couldn't imagine anything sexier than seeing Kratos' dark head between my legs. My eyes fluttered shut, and I arched into him, my body taking over from my mind.

"You like that?" He laughed low again then released my hands and moved down my body until his head was between my legs.

I couldn't answer him because I didn't want to admit that I did like it. I popped my eyes open again, because I really liked watching him spread my legs wide as he positioned himself between them.

Nothing covered me except for the skirts, which he deftly pulled to the side, emitting a choked groan as he stared down at me. He ran a finger between my folds and then slid it in his mouth. "Just as sweet as I knew you'd be."

I rolled my head back as he lowered his mouth to me, dragging his tongue up until he reached my clit. I sucked in a sharp breath, fisting the sheets.

"This is the little thing that makes you moan, Raisa?" he asked, his tone curious. I guessed other alien females didn't have one, but he'd clearly heard about them.

"Yes," I managed to say.

He swirled the tip of his tongue over it, and I bowed my back off the bed.

"Then I like this very much."

I felt like telling him he wasn't the only one, but my mouth didn't seem to work. But *his* sure did. I could only make soft keening noises as he continued to flick his tongue over my clit. My breathing became ragged, and my body writhed in response to his skillful tongue.

Kratos didn't stop, even when I wrapped my legs over his shoulders. He slid his hands under my ass, lifting me up and making my legs fall open wider. I grasped the back of his head, tangling my fingers in his long hair and holding his head to me as he sucked my clit and my body began to tremble.

I looked down, the sight of his long tail switching behind him making me moan even louder. There was no denying that the creature licking me was not a human, but I found that the thought of an alien warlord making me come with his tongue was enough to send me over the edge. As I quivered, he didn't stop his tongue's attentions, but instead slid one thick finger inside me, making me rear up off the bed and scream as my entire body spasmed, clenching his finger over and over until I sank back on the bed, gasping for breath.

Kratos sat back, wiping his mouth and looking down at me with hot eyes. Even though he still wore his kilt, his hard cock tented the leather folds. "Now you're ready for me, Raisa."

I was ready for him. My body throbbed from the need to have him inside me.

A heavy thudding on the door made him stiffen.

"Raas!" The voice on the other side called out. "You are needed on the command deck."

Kratos gritted his teeth, casting a glance over his shoulder. He glanced back down at me and sighed, tugging my skirts back over me so I was covered. Leaning down he brushed a kiss over my lips then gave me a sharp nip on my neck. "If I don't fuck you soon I might have to kill someone."

I watched him turn and stalk off. I was starting to feel the same way.

CHAPTER
SEVENTEEN

Kratos

"I apologize again for interrupting you, Raas." Bron walked briskly beside me as we headed down the steel corridors to the command deck.

My heart still pounded, and the sweet taste of the female lingered on my tongue, but I waved a hand in dismissal. "You said we have a captive?"

"We thought we should keep one alive for questioning. At least for now."

We both knew the captive would not live for long, but Bron was right to hold one for interrogation. "You were wise to summon me. I have a few questions for this mercenary."

The ship rumbled under my feet as we walked, and I was glad that we were once again in the air. There was safety for us in space, especially since we flew undetected.

We reached the command deck and crossed it quickly as

warriors clicked their heels in salute. Wide, iron doors slid open at the far side to reveal my battle chief's interrogation room, the *oblek*. Cramped, and even more shrouded in darkness than the command deck, the room held little but chains extending from the ceiling.

The Lussite captive hung by his arms from the chains, his head sagging forward as if he was asleep or dead. I hoped he was neither.

Corvak turned sharply when we entered. "Raas, I have been questioning this invader."

"Anything yet?" I asked, folding my arms over my chest and eyeing the creature's bare chest and the ridges that swept down from his neck to his shoulders.

Corvak twitched one shoulder. "Only that he is not the leader, and that their target was not the ship. Or us."

"I know." I walked toward the prisoner. "They were after my...the human female."

Bron's head swung toward me. "Why would Lussite mercenaries want a human female? How did they know about her?"

"The Zagrath," Corvak growled. "It could only be our enemy."

"It could have also been the humans we took her from," I said, bending down to look at the mercenary's bowed head. "Their captain in particular was not pleased with the deal the human made with me."

"I told you we should have killed them all," Corvak said, under his breath.

I spun on him. "Yes, cousin. I know what you said. But it is done."

He let out another noise that told me he clearly did not think the discussion over.

I unhooked my battle axe from my waist and used the end

to lift the captive's head so I could get a better look at his face. The ridges covering his forehead were smeared with blood and a purple bruise was blooming on his yellowed jaw. "The humans did not seem to be the type to interact with Lussites like this one. Besides, Lussites rarely leave this sector. How would they have intersected with the human freighter that was heading away from Vandar space?"

"So, it must have been the Zagrath," Corvak said. "The humans were working for them. They must have reported the abduction, and relayed information about our ship and us."

I let the alien's head drop. "You think the Zagrath hired these aliens?"

Bron rocked back on his heels. "They have used mercenaries against us before."

That was true. Our enemy had come at us with their imperial fleet but had also been known to employ hired guns to track us down.

"But if it was the Zagrath, why would they want to kill the human?" I asked.

"Kill her?" Bron stared at me. "Weren't they here to take her back?"

I gave a brusque shake of my head. "The female overheard them talking. Their instructions were to get her off our ship and dispose of her."

Corvak frowned at me. "She is sure? That does not make sense?"

"That is what she said." I walked around the dangling alien, assessing his dirty clothes.

"But Raas." Corvak dropped his voice. "She is a female. She could have lied to you."

I narrowed my gaze at him. "She did not lie."

"It makes no sense," Corvak repeated.

"It does if the Zagrath are trying to get to you, Raas," Bron said, locking eyes with me. "They have tracked you long enough to know that Vandar do not take captives. Perhaps they think that there is a reason you have claimed this female. They could be going after her to strike a blow to you."

I swallowed hard at this. Before, the thought of a female being taken from me would have been of no consequence. I had never become attached to one. No Vandar Raas did, until they surrendered their horde to a successor. But now...

"Raas barely knows this female." Corvak let out a rough laugh. "If the Zagrath think they will weaken us by killing one human, they do not know the Vandar as well as they should."

"Agreed," Bron said, his gaze flickering over me for a moment before he strode to the curved, floor-to-ceiling glass looking out onto the blackness of space. "But if the Zagrath believe the female is a point of weakness for our Raas, they will continue to come for her—and for us."

"Let them come." I pounded the end of my axe against the floor. "The Vandar do not fear the Zagrath. We have been hunting them for generations, and we will continue to hunt them until the empire is nothing but a wisp of a memory."

Corvak unhooked his own axe and thumped it on the floor. "Raas speaks the truth. It is we who hunt them and strike terror in the hearts of their soldiers. It is our raiders who strip their settlements and destroy their illegal outposts."

The Lussite moaned as he stirred, glancing up at us. His eyes went wide, and he yanked at the chains keeping him up.

"Are you ready to tell the Raas of the Vandar who ordered this attack?" Corvak advanced on him with his axe swinging by his side.

The alien's gaze darted to me, and his tongue licked his lips nervously. "I do not know. Our crew chief didn't tell us. Only that it was someone with a lot of power, and a lot of money."

"The Zagrath?" I pressed, holding his gaze with my own.

"Don't know." He shook visibly as Corvak walked behind him. "Could have been. They've got both of those."

"And you were tasked with taking the human off my ship and killing her?" I asked.

He twisted his head around to find Corvak, who stood behind him swinging his axe at his feet.

"Answer the Raas," Bron said, his voice hard.

The Lussite snapped his head back to mine. "That's right, but we might not have killed her right away." He gave me a leer that he probably meant to bond us as males. He had misjudged me.

"Anything else before we release you?" I asked, my skin prickling with the desire to add more bruises to the alien's body for what he'd suggested he and his mercenaries would have done to my female.

"That's all I know." He straightened up, clearly relieved that we would be releasing him.

I nodded, stepping back from him. "You should know that no one takes from the Vandar without punishment, especially not from the Raas."

I flicked my eyes to Corvak, whose tail slashed through the air behind him eagerly, and dipped my head almost imperceptibly. The Lussite's eyes flared with understanding only moments before my battle chief's axe severed his head from his body.

I bowed my head to him. "Well done, cousin."

Corvak straightened, wiping his bloody circular axe blade on his leather kilt. "That is only one soldier and one hunting party. If the Zagrath want her dead, they will keep coming. Do you not think her presence puts our ship at risk, Raas?"

I bristled at the challenge, but calmed myself. It was his job as my battle chief to warn of dangers. And we had learned that Astrid was a danger. "We do not fear the Zagrath, nor do we cater to their wants." I met his gaze. "We will fight them off like we always do."

"Yes, Raas." He clicked his heels sharply.

I turned and walked out of the *oblek* with Bron fast on my heels. When I'd almost reached the doors, he stepped in front of me. "Could I have a word, Raas?" He jerked his head toward my strategy room near the doors of the command deck.

"I always have time for my *majak*," I said, beckoning him to follow me into the private room.

Once we were inside and the doors had swished closed, I leaned against the ebony desk. "Say what is on your mind, Bron."

"May I speak freely, Raas?"

I crossed my legs at the ankles. "I would prefer it."

"You must be seen commanding. We have just been attacked. Word will spread quickly that it was because of the female. Your crew must see you leading them and not falling under her spell."

I straightened. "I am not under anyone's spell."

"I have known you a long time, Kratos. I have never seen you like this. It may not be a spell, but there is something about her that makes you different."

"Maybe she is the first thing I have not had to take by force and violence," I snapped, turning away from my *majak* and facing the windows.

"But you did take her."

I cannot tell him that I have still yet to claim the female.

That I am waiting until she comes to me. A Raas of the Vandar does not wait for any female. "Fine. I will stay on the command deck."

Bron let out a breath behind me.

I turned again, my arms crossing my bare chest. "But I want a guard on her. And someone to keep her company."

"Keep her company?" Bron's face creased with confusion.

"One of the apprentices. Assign our cleverest apprentice to be her companion when I am not with her."

"You think she will want to spend her time with a Vandar boy?"

"She will have no choice."

I twisted back around to look out at the black swath of sky. And I had no choice but to do whatever I had to, to protect what was mine.

EIGHTEEN

Astrid

He'd been gone for a while, but my heart had yet to regain its natural rhythm. I sat on the edge of the bed, trying not to replay what had happened, but having a hard time not thinking about how hard the Vandar Raas had made me come.

"Get a grip, Astrid," I said, grateful to hear my voice in the silent room. After the noises of the battle, the quiet humming of the ship's engines seemed almost too quiet. Not that I wanted to go through an attack like that again, but I didn't like being alone. Again.

I hummed to myself softly, the sound instantly calming me. *That was better,* I thought. *I'm not alone.*

The alternative to solitude was Kratos coming back. I rubbed my damp palms on the front of my dress. Was I really ready for that? My body seemed to think I was, as all my blood rushed south every time I thought about the huge alien with his head buried between my legs.

Even as my body heated at the memory, a part of me felt a twinge of guilt. I was not supposed to be giving myself so eagerly to my captor. I was supposed to be holding out in case my sister managed to mount a rescue. But did I even want to be rescued anymore? What would I really be going back to? A sad life on a junky freighter as the captain's incompetent sister?

I shook my head. I should not be having such ungrateful thoughts. Tara had done everything she could for me. It wasn't her fault that my talents didn't lie in space travel, and I'd sucked at every job she'd given me. I didn't know what I was good at, but it wasn't anything technical or mechanical.

I drew in a long breath. Did I really think being a captive of the Vandar was a better life than the one I'd had with my sister? It had certainly been more exciting, so far. And I liked being wanted by someone. On Tara's ship, no one had any use for me.

Sure, the Raas was intense, and I was in serious danger of losing my virginity to him, but what was I holding onto it for, anyway?

"It's not like anyone else wanted it." At least no one I'd been interested in. The awkward systems hacker on my sister's ship who didn't take enough showers did *not* count.

The more time I spent with the dark, dangerous Vandar, the harder it was to remember why I kept saying no. Not when he made me feel the way he did, and not when he was so good with his tongue.

I couldn't help giggling to myself, slapping a hand over my mouth when the door swished open. I leapt to my feet, expecting Kratos to stalk into the room. But it was not Kratos, it was one of his warriors and a young boy.

"Can I help you?" I eyed both of them.

The Vandar raider inclined his head slightly. "I am Bron, the *majak* of the Raas."

"*Majak*?"

"His most trusted warrior. His second in command."

"Oh, you're his first officer."

He tilted his head at me. "If that is what humans call it. The Raas asked me to check on you. He's been detained on the command deck."

I tried to mask my disappointment. "Do you know when he'll be back?"

"It might be a while. There is much to do after an attack."

"Of course." I had a feeling this *majak* knew that the attack had been all about me.

"Raas has assigned a guard outside the room, and this attendant to keep you company." He put a hand on the boy's back and pushed him forward. The young Vandar wore a kilt similar to the raider warriors, but it was made from a thick, dark cloth, instead of leather. The belt around his waist was also cloth, with a small dagger attached to it instead of a giant battle axe.

I eyed the boy and his flushed cheeks. "Keep me company?"

Bron took a step back. "He did not want to leave you alone again. Krin will keep you company until the Raas returns."

Before I could argue with this plan, Bron had left the room. The boy named Krin stared at the closed door as if willing it to open again. It was obvious that the kid had as little say in the Raas's scheme as I did.

For a second, I wanted to run after Bron and tell him

that I didn't need a babysitter, and certainly not a prepubescent boy. Then I glanced down at the child with dark, tousled hair and a twitching tail. He might just be a kid, but he was a Vandar kid. Maybe it wouldn't be such a bad thing to spend some more time with someone who knew Kratos. Or at least knew more about him than I did.

"Come on in," I said. "Are you hungry?"

He looked up at me with big, brown eyes. "I don't think I'm supposed to eat your food."

I fluttered a hand as I walked toward the dining table. The domes still covered the dinner that Kratos and I hadn't finished. I was sure some of the food wouldn't be good cold, but there must be some sort of dessert I could use to tempt Krin.

"If you're my attendant, then I think I should get to make the rules, right?"

He shrugged, but I saw a smile tease the corners of his mouth.

"And I think you must be hungry." I reached the table and started lifting the heavy metal domes off the plates. "Does anything look good to you?"

His eye were round when I revealed a bowl filled with knots of bread. "I like those."

I pointed to a bench and put the bowl in front of it. "Have as many as you want."

Sitting down next to him, I watched him devour at least three of the bread knots before he paused for a breath.

"You sure you don't want one?" he asked.

I shook my head. "They're all yours. I'm guessing you don't eat as well as the Raas?"

He gave me a look that told me he thought I might be simple. "No one eats like the Raas. But he's the Raas."

"And what's your job on the ship?" I'd never heard of young boys on Vandar raider ships.

"I'm an apprentice," he said through a mouthful. "It's an honor to be picked to learn how to be a raider. Then when we get old enough—if we're good enough—we can join our own raider horde."

"What about your families?"

"Some of us don't have any, but the rest of us leave our families on the Vandar settlements."

My heart squeezed. "Do you ever see them again?"

"Sure, we do. The hordes visit the settlements, and then when we're done being raiders, we go back and live there."

I'd never heard of Vandar settlements. Then again, there was a lot about the Vandar that was a mystery to me.

"But no females ever fly with your hordes?" I asked.

He met my eyes, then looked down, shaking his head. "Never."

"What do you think about the Raas bringing me on board, Krin?"

The boy shrugged again. "He's the Raas. He can do whatever he wants." He peeked at me from under long lashes any woman would covet. "And you're pretty enough that any male would like you to warm his bed, even if you don't have a tail. At least, that's what the crew says."

I tried not to be offended that the Vandar crew was discussing me warming all of their beds—and my lack of a tail. "Is the crew upset I'm here?"

"Not as long as you don't make our Raas go soft." He tore a knot of bread into two pieces. "Humans are too soft."

"And tail-less," I added with a grin.

He returned my smile. "That, too."

Knowing a little of the violent history of Earth, I wasn't so sure about humans being soft, but I didn't argue with him.

"I promise not to make your Raas soft. I cannot imagine someone as fierce as him ever being soft."

A smile spread across the boy's face. "He's the toughest Raas there is. Even tougher than his father. They say one of his brothers shows little mercy, but our Raas has more victories."

"His brothers also lead their own hordes of ships?"

Krin held up two fingers. "Two of them. I don't know how much Raas likes them, though."

"Brothers often fight amongst themselves. So do sisters."

"You have a brother or a sister?" the boy asked me.

"A sister," I said, my throat thickening. "We didn't fight too much."

The boy reached hand up and touched my hair. "Is she as pretty as you?"

"Prettier."

The boy scrunched up his nose as if he didn't believe me. "Well, I still like you best."

I laughed. Vandar were nothing if not loyal. "I imagine an apprentice as clever as you must know everything about this ship, right?"

He puffed out his chest. "Just about."

I flicked my eyes to the food on the table. "I have a hard time believing that Vandar don't eat dessert. How about you take me to the kitchens, and we find something sweet?"

NINETEEN

Kratos

I leaned on the console as I peered over Corvak's shoulder. "Still nothing?"

The command deck hummed with activity, the warriors alert as our horde flew in hunting formation on the lookout for Zagrath ships. Even though I could not see the other black warbirds flanking us out the front of the ship, I knew they were there, flying invisibly. I heard the chatter of incoming transmissions from my horde ship captains, and the beeping of our sensors as they scanned space.

"We have not been hunting that long, Raas." There was impatience in my battle chief's voice, which I ignored.

I knew he was right. We had only been scouring the sector since second watch, but I'd been sure we would have come across some Zagrath ships by now. Deals were not made with low-tech mercenaries like the Lussites without some contact, so it only made sense that there would be some Zagrath activity near Jaldon. So far, we had come up empty.

"We should move closer to the neutral territory," my battle chief said. "We will find Zagrath there for sure."

"I do not want to destroy Zagrath ships for sport." I gripped the hard edge of the console tight in frustration. "I need to know who is behind this plot."

Corvak watched me as I scraped a hand through my hair. "Has our mission changed, Raas? Do we no longer hunt down all Zagrath?"

I growled low. I hated being called out by my cousin, and especially in front of my crew. I drew myself up to my full height and looked down on him. "You know very well that no one despises the Zagrath as much as I do. But it does not serve my purpose to blow them all out of the sky before determining that they are, indeed, behind the cowardly attack on our ship and my property."

Corvak's eyes shifted down for a moment before meeting mine again. "Who else, Raas?"

I spun away from him and stared out the wide glass front of the ship. "That is what I must know."

"Raas," Bron called from where he stood at a nearby console. "You should see this."

I took long steps to reach him, standing shoulder to shoulder with my *majak* as I focused on the star chart illuminating the screen. "What do you see?"

"It is not about the Zagrath. Not directly, but I thought you would be interested to know about the path of the freighter we took your captive from."

I narrowed my eyes at the blue dot he'd highlighted and its trajectory since we'd intercepted it. "It has not continued on its original route?"

Bron shook his head. "It appears to be flying in a search pattern."

"You think it's looking for us?" I let out a laugh. "That sad freighter thinks it can track down a Vandar raider horde flying unseen?"

"The female captain appeared to be headstrong and lacking in prudence."

I slid my eyes to Bron. "You show great restraint, *majak*."

He shrugged. "She seems to be brave. I will give the stubborn female that much."

I looked again at the path of the freighter as it skirted Vandar territory. "Or incredibly stupid." I shook my head. "I cannot concern myself with a ship that will never find us. Right now, I must focus on finding out who would dare board my ship and try to take what is mine." I dropped my voice. "The female was fine when you left her with the apprentice?"

He inclined his head at me. "Yes, Raas. Although I am not sure the boy was such a good idea."

"Why not?"

Bron hesitated, as if considering whether or not to tell me. "I asked the guard I posted outside your quarters to report directly to me."

"Yes? Is there a problem?"

"Not so much a problem, Raas." Bron pressed his lips together briefly. "But the human and her apprentice are no longer in your quarters."

"What?" Panic fluttered in my chest. The same panic I'd felt when I'd run into my room and found Astrid missing. "And you did not think it was a problem that my female was missing?"

"She is not missing. She and the boy are in the kitchens."

I blinked a few times, not sure I'd heard correctly. "The kitchens? Of this ship? Why is she there?"

"From what I understand, she and the boy are looking for something she calls 'dessert.'"

"Why did the guard let them out of my quarters in the first place?" I fisted my hands by my side.

"From what I understand, they were very convincing." Bron locked his gaze on mine. "It is not like she can escape from a moving ship, Raas. She cannot fly our ships. If she is still your captive and there is any danger of her wanting to escape, that is. If she is more than that, you should consider giving her some freedoms."

I glared at my *majak*, hating the truth in his words. "I do not need advice on what to do with the female." I turned abruptly, my kilt slapping my thighs. "I will handle this myself. You have the command deck."

I walked off without a backward glance, my long legs eating up the floor as I made my way quickly through the ship. Whether she was able to leave the ship or not, I could not have the female wandering freely around a raider warbird. For one, she belonged in my quarters with me. I wanted to find her there when I returned from the command deck. And for another, there were no females on Vandar ships for a reason. I did not want my crew coveting what belonged to me, even though the dress she wore hid her curves well.

I pounded down a spiraling iron staircase, leaping down the last two steps and landing hard on the floor. Blood ran hot through my veins as I thought of other male eyes on Astrid. I'd never had any problem sharing females before, since most of my encounters had been with pleasurers. But they were not her, and they had not been mine. Even though I was drawn to the inner steel she didn't know she had, it was her soft curves and innocence that fired my need to protect her. She was my opposite in every way, and I craved the balance she brought out in me.

When I reached the arched opening that led into the kitchen, I paused outside to catch my breath and quell my temper. I wanted to scold her, not terrify her.

"You've never had cake before?" Astrid's voice rose above the throaty rumble of the engines.

"What's cake?" Another voice asked, and I knew it must be the apprentice who'd been assigned to her.

I peeked quickly around the doorframe and saw the pair standing at a long steel table. I ducked back so they wouldn't see me. I knew my intention had been to drag her back to my quarters, but I was curious. I wanted to hear more about this cake.

Astrid laughed. "It's something sweet and delicious that you eat for special occasions, like birthdays."

"Birthdays?"

"Don't tell me Vandar don't celebrate birthdays." She huffed out a breath. "So, you've never had a birthday cake?"

"No," the boy said. "Do you get an entire cake each time you have a birthday?"

"Of course, but you only have a birthday once a year to celebrate the day you were born."

"Why would you celebrate being born? That's not an achievement." The Vandar boy sounded as confused as I was. This human tradition sounded very odd.

"You don't need an achievement to celebrate," Astrid said. "Everyone should be celebrated just for being."

"You are not Vandar," the boy grumbled. "We celebrate when one is inducted into the raiders, or after a very large battle. Not for simply being born."

Astrid laughed again. "You aren't going to ruin birthdays

for me, Krin. When I was growing up, my parents made birthdays a really big deal. They had presents for us, balloons everywhere, and any flavor of cake we wanted. It was the one day we could do whatever we wanted."

"That does sound fun," Krin said, his resolve clearly wavering.

"It was the best." Astrid's voice trailed off, and she cleared her throat. "But that was a long time ago, and I haven't had a birthday cake in years."

"Maybe we could make one, even though it isn't anyone's birthday."

"That's a great idea, Krin. And since we don't know when your birthday is, it could be yours, right?"

"I guess so."

Astrid clapped her hands. "Since you've never had one before, this will officially be your first birthday cake."

I looked around the corner again and saw her digging through some cabinets and handing things out to the shaggy-haired boy, who was smiling widely. I took a few steps back and leaned against the corridor wall.

My anger had evaporated as I'd listened to her talk about her past and the unusual, human tradition of birthdays. I no longer had the urge to drag her back and throw her in my quarters. Strangely, I wanted to let her make her cake.

I blew out a breath as I walked back to the command deck, hoping this did not mean what I was afraid it did.

No Raas could afford to go soft. Not unless he wanted to sign his own death warrant.

CHAPTER
TWENTY

Kratos

Heaving in a breath, I peered around the empty battle ring. The only sounds were the vibrating of the ship beneath my feet and my own heavy breathing. I swiped the back of my hand across my slick forehead and then across my damp chest, flinging the droplets of sweat to the floor.

My muscles were twitching from the exertion, but my head was no longer so muddled. I was still Raas, no matter how I felt for the human. And I had still destroyed more Zagrath ships than any other Raas.

When the metal cage rattled, I spun around with my axe high. When I saw who was outside, I let my weapon sag. "Corvak. Do you bring news of the Zagrath?"

"Nothing yet, Raas." He eyed me. "I heard you were working out and thought I'd join you."

I tilted my head at him. I had not sparred with my cousin in a very long time. It was usually my *majak* who got in the ring with me. "You wish to fight your Raas?"

He pushed open the door and stepped in with me. "Perhaps my Raas needs a challenge."

There was a new edge to his words. I held out one hand, flicking my fingers toward myself. "*Vaes*, cousin. Show me what you've got."

He gave me a menacing grin, unhooking his own axe from his waist and swinging it by his legs. "Gladly, Kratos."

Even though we were kin, Corvak rarely called me by my given name. Despite being cousins, we were not as close as Bron and I were. There had always been a distance between me and my battle chief. I didn't know if it was because of the bad blood between our fathers, or if my advancement to the rank of Raas—along with my two brothers'—had caused him to hold me at arm's length.

It had never bothered me before. He'd always done his job well, and a Raas did not require affection from his crew. But now, as I watched him advance toward me, I wondered what my cousin really thought of me. And whether he would be happier if I was no longer Raas—or no longer alive.

"I take it we will have no need for the sparring axes?" I asked, seeing the gleam of his blade.

"We will not." With a roar, he lunged for me and swung his axe at my head. I ducked, diving across the cage and leaping to my feet with my own weapon raised.

Corvak was already charging me. I swung my blade at him, barely missing his ear as he parried to one side, spinning and attempting to come around behind me.

I spun with him, my axe following the rotation of my

body and making contact with the curve of his blade. The impact reverberated up my arm and made me stagger back.

"You have something you wish to tell me, Corvak?" I asked, when he also stumbled back.

"I have told you what I think," he panted, his face already flaming red. "You refuse to hear me."

"Tell me again," I growled. "What do you think?"

He tossed his axe handle from one hand to the other as he stared me down. "You are letting that female influence you."

"Untrue," I said, squeezing the handle of my weapon. "I do everything I do to protect the Vandar."

"And protect her," he spit out.

"She is mine to protect." My words were low and deadly. "I took her as my prize. A Raas takes what he wants, and no one will harm what is mine."

"That whore will be the end of us." Corvak's voice rose to a shout. "She rules you, and she rules the horde."

Rage bubbled up as I charged him, slamming my body into his and knocking his axe from his grip. "No one rules my horde but me, and no one questions my loyalty to it!"

Corvak hit the floor hard, and I pinned him down with the long handle of my axe across his throat and my legs pinning his arms to his side. He flailed under me, one arm trying to reach for his axe lying not far from him.

"You would take up your axe and strike me down, cousin?" I asked, leaning my face down over his. "That is how you show loyalty to your Raas?"

His eyes flashed as he looked up at me, then his body went limp and his eyes closed. "Forgive me, Raas."

I stood, picking up his axe and holding both weapons as he stood up. His chest heaved as he drew in breaths.

"If you ever question my loyalty to my horde again,

Corvak, I will put you out an air lock." My voice was little more than a hiss. "After I cut off your head."

"I was wrong to question you, Raas." He did not look up. "But I do not understand why we do not kill these Zagrath."

"You do not need to understand." I threw his axe at him. "Raas does not need to explain himself to anyone. Not even to his battle chief."

His head snapped up. "Am I still your battle chief?"

I studied him for a moment, wondering if I *should* put him out an airlock, since dissent could spread through a crew like a virus.

"For now," I finally said, turning and stomping from the battle ring. I stopped at the bottom of the steps, turning and pointing to him with my blade. "Do not mistake my mercy for weakness. If you do, it will be the last miscalculation you make."

He clicked his heels together and jutted his chin up. "Yes, Raas."

My heart was hammering wildly as I stormed through the ship to my quarters. Corvak was right about one thing. I could not let any female rule me.

A Raas did not make deals. A Raas took what he wanted when he wanted it. It was time the female learned that.

TWENTY-ONE

Astrid

I felt his weight on the bed as the movement pulled me out of sleep. I'd sent Krin back to his own quarters a while ago, knowing that Kratos would return and not welcome a young boy curled up like a puppy at the end of his bed.

We'd managed to make a passable birthday cake, and Krin had devoured it like he was a child tasting sugar for the first time, his enthusiasm making me forget everything about where I was and how conflicted I felt about the Vandar, and the Raas who made my heart race.

Rolling over, I blinked a few times to bring my eyes into focus in the dark. Then I sat up quickly once my eyes locked on him. Kratos stood completely naked at the foot of the bed, one knee on the bed and his cock jutting out rigid from his body. His chest rose and fell as if he'd run all the way to his quarters, and his body glistened with sweat.

"Are you okay?" I asked. "Did something happen?"

He yanked the silk sheets off me, revealing a shorter nightgown I'd selected from the clothes brought to me. His gaze went to my mostly bare legs, and he let out a low rumble. "I have been patient enough, Raisa."

He grabbed my ankles and pulled me down to him in a single fast motion, the gown riding up to my waist.

I tried to tug it down again, but he pushed my hands away and tore the silky fabric completely off my body.

"What do you think you're doing?" I cried, even though there wasn't much doubt in my mind exactly what was happening.

He took my hands and pinned them over my head. "What I should have done the first second I was alone with you. What I have wanted to do since I saw you on that ship." He lowered his head, so it was next to mine, inhaling deeply. "I'm claiming you as mine, female. From this moment on, you will be the property of Raas Kratos of the Vandar. No one else can lay a finger on you. And no one else can ever fuck you."

My heart beat like a trip wire as I struggled to loosen my hands. His body pressed hard against mine, making my breaths ragged. His own breath was hot against my neck, sending spasms of unwanted pleasure through me as I arched back.

"You cannot escape me, Raisa." He nipped my throat between words. "You are mine. Do you understand?"

My thighs were slick, as heat pulsed hot between my legs, and I cursed my body for its traitorous response. I shook my head but didn't speak.

"I know you understand." He murmured, his voice softer

as it buzzed my ear. "You've always been mine, haven't you? You've always been waiting for me? That's why there were no other males before. You were destined for me."

He held both my wrists together with one of his hands and moved his other down one side of my now-bare body. Even though his hands were huge, he wasn't rough as his fingers skimmed the swell of my breast. Lifting his head from my neck, he met my gaze, his own eyes black and shining. "Tell me."

My pulse skittered, and my throat was so dry I could only make a high, breathy sound.

The Vandar warlord used his knees to part my legs, his cock hard against my thighs. "*Tvek.*" His eyes rolled back in his head for a moment, and he bit down on his bottom lip. "You're already soaking for me."

My cheeks burned. I couldn't believe how wet I was, or that I actually wanted this huge alien to fuck me. But I did.

"Tell me you want me," he insisted, when he'd locked eyes with me again. "I can feel how much you need me. You don't have to fight it, Raisa. You don't have to fight me."

So many emotions stormed through me I was sure I'd implode. But he was right. I didn't have the strength to resist him anymore, or fight my own feelings. "I want you, Raas."

His pupils flared, and he crushed his mouth to mine, parting my lips with a hard swipe of his tongue. Our tongues tangled, and he moaned into my mouth as he kissed me deeper. When he relaxed his grip on my hands, I wrapped them around his broad back, then moved them into his hair.

His kiss was so drugging, I was only faintly aware that he'd moved his hand down and was dragging the crown of his cock through my folds. I curled one leg around his ass, and he groaned. He tore his mouth from mine, breath hitching in his throat as he notched his cock at my opening, holding it there.

My heart was knocking against my ribs, and my entire body trembled, but I didn't want him to stop.

"Raisa." He stroked a finger down one cheek, his voice husky.

"Please," I whispered. "I want you inside me."

He put his forehead to mine as he pushed his cock in slowly. The stretch made my breath catch in my throat as my body tried to take him. He paused, lifting himself to lock eyes with me. "I'm sorry, Raisa."

Before I could ask him why he was sorry, he'd thrust himself the rest of the way in with a single powerful stroke. I gasped at the searing pain and dug my fingernails into his back, tears springing to my eyes.

Burying his head in my neck, he murmured words in Vandar to me as the pain faded.

After a minute or so, I unclenched my nails. "You can move, Raas."

Raising himself to his elbows, he dragged his cock slowly out and back in, his neck muscles tight from the restraint. "So tight."

Even though I was still adjusting to his massive cock, I loved the feeling of being filled by him. I shifted my hips up to meet his, and his pupils widened again. "You like it deep?"

I nodded. "I want more."

He dragged his thumb across my mouth, putting it between my lips. I sucked on it, and he grinned. "Greedy Raisa." He sat back on his heels, lifting my hips with his hands and spreading my legs wider. Looking down, he let out a dark growl. "Your tight little *kurlek* looks so perfect with my cock splitting it."

"Kurlek?" I managed to ask as slid his thick length into me again.

Kratos moved a finger to my clit and circled it as he continued to stroke his cock deep. "Your cunt, Raisa. Your perfect little cunt."

Hearing that word on his lips made me bow my back and let out my own moan.

"You like that word better though, don't you?" he growled.

I could only gasp in response, my release building as the Vandar warlord pounded into me, his finger stroking my clit.

"Say you're mine, Raisa," he said between gasps.

I looked at him, his expression wild and his dark hair a torrent around his face. "I'm yours."

He thrust harder, his jaw tight. "You belong to Raas Kratos." He circled my clit faster. "No one else will ever fuck you but me. Promise me!"

"I promise," I said, my words slurred as my legs began to shake and my body pulsed around his cock. I raked my hand through my own hair and screamed until my throat was hoarse. He didn't stop hammering into me as I came and moments later, he was thrusting hard and arching his back as he shot into me.

Wrapping both legs around his waist, I pulled him down onto me. Kratos rolled onto his back, taking me with him, his cock still very much inside me. I lay my head on his damp chest, rising and falling with him as he caught his breath. After a few minutes, he took my head in his hands and lifted it so that he could meet my eyes.

"Are you okay, Raisa?" He smoothed a strand of hair off my forehead. "Did it hurt too much?"

"Not too much," I said, although I could already feel the

painful throb between my legs. I bit my lip, shy to ask my next question.

"Was it okay for you?" I whispered, despising the shake in my voice. "I mean, since I'd never..."

He pulled me up so that my face was over his. "It was perfect. You are perfect." His hand cupped my jaw. "And you are mine."

CHAPTER
TWENTY-TWO

Kratos

She wiggled on top of me, and I wrapped my tail around her hips to still her movements. Her brow furrowed.

"If you continue to move like that, I will have to fuck you again," I said, my voice a low rumble. My cock was still inside her tight heat and her movements were making it stiffen again.

"Oh." She looked surprised, but then her lips curled into a small smile. "I wouldn't mind that so much."

I tilted my head at her, amazed that one who had been so shy was now so hungry for me. "You are sure you will not be sore?"

"Oh, I definitely will be, but I don't mind so much." She pushed herself up so she was straddling me, her hands braced on my chest.

I moved my grip on her hips up to cup her round breasts, rolling the hard points between my fingers and thumbs. "Everything about you is soft, except for these."

She let out a moan and tilted her head back as she moved herself up and down my cock slowly. As much as I wanted to flip her onto her back and thrust myself deep, I forced myself to let her ride me as I watched.

Her eyelids fluttered as she leaned forward, letting her hair fall forward and brush across my chest muscles. She dug her fingers into my flesh as her pace increased, and when she opened her eyes to lock onto mine, she was breathing hard and looked almost desperate.

I moved my hands back down to her hips, lifting her up until the crown of my cock teased her opening and then bringing her down again. She gasped with each deep thrust, clawing at my chest before she reared up and arched her back, shaking as she spasmed around my cock.

I sat up and flipped her over until she was on her hands and knees. She was still sucking in breath when I forced her head down onto the bed and tilted her ass up, spreading her legs and plunging inside her.

Tvek, she was so tight it was hard not to explode with each stroke.

Looking down at her curvy ass, I loved how her flesh quivered as I pounded into her. So soft and perfect. I grasped her hips, angling them so I could go even deeper, then I leaned forward and pulled her hands back, holding them at the small of her back while I fucked her.

"Do you like this?" I gritted out as my release chased me.

She twisted her head to look back at me, her eyes molten. "Yes, Raas."

"Then you will like this more." I curled my tail around so that the tip could flick her little bundle of nerves while I took her from behind. As the silky fur found her slick nub, she gasped and jerked, her body trembling once more.

"Do you like my tail playing with you, Raisa?" I rasped, savoring the sensation of fucking her while my tail stroked her slickness.

She bobbed her head up and down without speaking. But her body told me everything I needed to know as her tight heat spasmed around my cock and her gasps were high and breathy.

I let out a primal roar as I hammered home and gave one final hard thrust, emptying into her, hot and hard. She sank onto the bed, and I collapsed beside her, tugging her so that her body was tucked into mine. The only sounds in the room were that of our frantic breath.

"You are still okay?" I asked, once I could speak again.

She hitched in a breath. "I might never walk again."

I eyed the top of her head. "You are sure you were a virgin?"

"Yes." Her voice was hesitant. "I think I'd remember doing something like *that* before."

Although I believed her—I'd felt how unimaginably tight she'd been—it was hard to reconcile the tentative virgin with the woman who'd just ridden my cock with such fervor.

She lifted her head to look at me. "Why?"

"You do not fuck like a virgin."

Her cheeks immediately flooded with color. "I guess I just really liked it. Was I not supposed to?"

"No, you were." I rubbed a hand along her back. "I suppose I am feeling lucky that I captured such a lusty human."

She nudged me hard, giggling. "If you didn't use your tail, I might have been able to control myself."

"Oh, I do not want you controlling yourself. And I am

glad you enjoyed my tail. Just one more reason you are meant to be mine, Raisa."

She dropped her gaze to my chest. "I don't think your crew agrees with you."

"My crew has no say in the matter," I bit out, more harshly than I'd intended. "I am Raas. I answer to no one."

"But they're not happy I'm here, right? They don't like having a woman on board."

I looked down at her, but her eyes were fixed on my chest where she was tracing the curve of my markings. "Who told you that?"

"No one had to tell me. I can feel the mood on the ship. It's pretty obvious."

Feel the mood? Was this a human thing? "What do you feel?"

She twitched one shoulder up. "For one, your first officer is fine with me, but he's worried about you and about what the crew thinks. He wants to protect you."

I narrowed my gaze at her soft, pale hair. "Bron is my most loyal warrior, but how do you know all that about him?"

"It's a sense I got when he was talking to me. The way he looked at me, the way he said your name. Little things. But it's usually the little things that give people away." She drew in a long breath. "Like on my sister's ship—the one you took me from—I always knew that the crew tolerated me only because my sister was the captain. They were nice to my face, but the smiles were never real. Not that I blame them. They'd earned their spots, but I'd just been given one because of my sister, and I was pretty bad at it. I mean, obviously, since I navigated us into Vandar space."

I was suddenly very grateful that Astrid had been so bad at her job. "What do you sense about my other warriors?"

"I haven't exactly met many, but the one who was by your side when you brought me on your ship…"

"If it wasn't Bron, you must mean Corvak, my battle chief."

"He envies you," she said. "He wants what you have. Well, maybe not me. He isn't crazy about me." Her finger tracing my markings paused. "You should be careful with that one."

Her observation about Corvak was painfully accurate, but I did not like getting a warning from a female. I shook my head. "He would never be disloyal."

"Especially not if he feels appreciated. You could diffuse his jealousy by making him more important. Or feel more important. Then he wouldn't be tempted to betray you."

I clenched my jaw at the casual way she talked about treason. "More important than battle chief?"

She shrugged. "I don't know. I just sense he needs to feel important."

I reminded myself that humans did not understand the Vandar ways, and that females—even a Raisa—did not contradict a Raas. But she did not know, and I was enjoying hearing her impressions of my crew too much to shut her up. Or maybe it was just the sound of her voice. I took a deep breath. "Have you always known what people think?"

She laughed. "It's not like I'm psychic. I can't read minds, but I guess I do read faces and those little flashes of expressions that people try to hide. And, yeah, I've been doing it for as long as I can remember. It used to drive my parents crazy because they could never bluff me."

"Your parents are…?"

"Gone," she said quickly. "For a while now. It's just been me and Tara since I was around twelve and she was fifteen."

"Two females by themselves?" The thought of it was startling. Vandar females—especially ones so young—would never be alone. Then again, our race had maintained our horde structure—in space and on our hidden settlements. We lived and moved as a group. No one was left behind or made to fend for themself. And no female would not be protected by a male. Or a horde of them.

"We were living on an outpost when my parents were killed. There wasn't anyone to take care of us, so Tara took charge. She's always been good at that. She's also good at cards. It's how she won her ship."

"And started working for the Zagrath?"

Her small body tensed on mine. "You don't know what it's like trying to survive out there. If the empire is the only one paying, you work for them."

"Even if they take over planets and rule civilizations that are not theirs?" My pulse quickened. "Even if they control entire sectors without mercy?"

She lifted her head and looked at me. "Is a Vandar raider lecturing me on mercy?"

I clenched my teeth. I knew our reputation as merciless and brutal was deserved, but it was for a higher purpose. "We are only merciless to those who are part of the empire."

"That includes a lot of innocent people."

I stared up at the ceiling. "No one who works for the empire is innocent. Every act that benefits them means fewer planets are free."

"So, was I guilty? And my sister? And all the decent people working on her ship just trying to scrape out a living?"

I grunted but did not look down at her, even though I felt her intense gaze on me. "I showed mercy on your sister and her ship." I dropped my eyes to hers. "And to you."

"But if you hadn't wanted to take me...?"

"Do not ask me questions you don't want the answers to,

Raisa." I sat up, letting her fall to the bed, as I swung my legs over the side and stood. I stalked to the dresser, pulling out a dark swath of fabric I wrapped around my waist.

"Why are you so mad?" she asked.

I spun around, taking fast steps toward her. She'd sat up and pulled the black sheets around her chest, but she scooted back when she saw me coming, her head bumping the headboard of iron shields and axes.

"I am angry because the Zagrath invaded my planet and decimated my people, ruling over us with cruelty until those who were left revolted and took to the skies. Because we fought back and continue to challenge them, we are the evil ones. We, who only want to free the galaxy from the empire's choking control, are called terrorists while they move freely as legitimate rulers."

She gaped at me. "I didn't know."

I folded my arms and let out a choked laugh. "The Zagrath have done a very good job of painting us as criminals. Our only wish is to free the galaxy."

She blinked her wide, green eyes at me. "And then? What happens if you finally win? What will the raider hordes do then?"

It was my turn to stare at her. I did not know what would happen then. I had been raiding for most of my life, and the Vandar had been raiding for generations. I could not imagine a world in which I was not fueled by my need for revenge and justice.

"Your life should be about more than revenge, Kratos."

I bent over her, my face so close to hers I could feel her quick breath. I ran a hand up her neck, closing it around her throat. "You are here to warm my bed and pleasure me, female, but I do not want you in my head."

TWENTY-THREE

Astrid

Kratos was gone when I woke up the next morning, and I didn't see him for the entire day. I guessed I'd freaked him out by hitting too close to home. I wasn't trying to get in his head—like he'd accused me of doing—but I knew there was more to the guy than muscles and rage.

When he crawled in bed that night, he woke me up by pushing my nightgown up and climbing on top of me. I'd still been half asleep when he'd thrust his cock into me, moving hard and fast in the dark. Even though he didn't speak as he fucked me, he'd kissed me deeply, his tongue caressing mine as he moved thickly between my legs.

"Raas," I'd whispered, when he'd broken the kiss.

He shook his head, kissing me again. "Don't talk. I just want to feel you, Raisa."

Then he'd kept his mouth on mine, silencing me with his intoxicating kisses. Even when I'd come, moaning and jerking underneath him, he'd swallowed my cries with his mouth. But there had been so much in his kisses—so much longing, so much need, so much pain.

After he'd roared his release and pulsed hot into me, he'd held me for a while, kissing my neck and face before rolling over and holding me to him as he fell asleep.

And so it went, day after day. He would leave before I woke, stay away all day, then crawl into bed, spreading my legs and taking me. There were few words, only loud gasps and moans and screams and, finally, panting and the heavy breathing of his sleep. Sometimes I fell asleep right away, sometimes I stayed awake and listened to him breathe, wondering what my life had become.

I hated to admit that I loved sex with my Vandar captor as much as I did. But I also knew I needed more than our encounters in the dark. It was clear that the Raas was avoiding me, but the strange wall he'd built between us left me with an ache in my heart. Even when he was inside me, his cock filling me completely, I felt the emptiness of our unspoken words. The way he touched me and licked me and kissed me made me feel adored, but that feeling disappeared during the long hours he left me alone with only Krin for company.

Krin, on the other hand, had become much more to me than I could have imagined. After our venture into the kitchens, he'd gotten permission to take me around the ship, so at least I was no longer confined to the Raas' quarters.

"What should we do today?" he asked when he arrived at my door, his smile wide and his dark hair as messy as it always was.

I waved him inside. I'd already bathed and eaten the

breakfast brought to me, but I'd saved some of the bread for my young friend—like always. I motioned to the two brown knots on the low table, and he eagerly snatched them up, perching on the ottoman as he took a bite. I didn't think they underfed the apprentices, but I also knew that growing boys were always hungry.

"Well, we've probably bothered the kitchen staff enough for this week." I watched his face fall. "But I promise I'll make you another cake soon. Maybe this time I can figure out how to make icing."

"Icing?" he mumbled through his mouthful.

I laughed. "It's sweet and sticky and supposed to cover the outside of a cake."

Krin wrinkled his nose and swallowed. "Why would you want to put something sticky all over a cake?'

He had a good point. "I don't know. It's really sweet and tastes amazing. And you can't steal bits of frosting off the top, if there's no frosting."

He seemed to accept this explanation. "We could celebrate your birthday next and put icing on that cake."

"My birthday isn't for a while, although I'm starting to lose track of time." I walked to the wide windows across the far wall and peered out at the black curtain of space, tiny pinpricks of light dotting it.

He scrunched his mouth to one side. "How old are you?"

"Twenty Earth years. Not very old." I could tell from his face he wasn't so sure.

"The Raas is older than you." Krin always looked solemn when he spoke of Kratos. "He has been leading this horde for many rotations, and even more battles."

"How often does the horde do battle?" I asked, turning away from the view. As far as I knew, we'd been patrolling for days without contact with any other ships.

He bobbled his head. "Depends. Sometimes a lot. Sometimes not."

I folded my arms over my chest. "Very helpful, Krin."

He laughed then slapped a hand over his mouth, glancing back at the door as if the guard outside could hear through the thick metal.

"I have an idea," I said, walking closer to where he sat and lowering my voice to a conspiratorial whisper.

His eyes lit up with excitement. Like any child, he was fascinated by anything secret or forbidden. I planned to use that to my advantage.

"If we go into battle, every Vandar knows how to defend himself, right?"

He nodded with enthusiasm. "Of course."

"Even the apprentices are instructed in basic combat as part of their training, yes?"

"Yes." He puffed out his chest. "We all know how to fight."

"Then doesn't it seem like I should learn how to fight? If I'm going to live on a Vandar raider warship, I should at least know the basics of how to defend myself, don't you think?"

Krin gnawed on his bottom lip. "First of all, our ships are warbirds. And I don't know about teaching you to battle. The Raas may not want you doing that."

"The Raas isn't here," I said, then realized how sharp my tone had been. "I mean, the Raas is busy leading the horde. He can't be bothered teaching me how to fight. But you can."

Krin did not look convinced.

"Do you remember when attackers invaded the ship on Jaldon?" I asked. "I was all by myself, and I had no way to protect myself. I didn't have a weapon and even if I'd found one, I didn't know how to use it. I had to run and hide. If the Raas hadn't found me before the invaders did…" The crack in my voice was real, the memory of huddling alone, terrified of being found by the aliens who wanted to kill me, still fresh in my mind.

"Okay," Krin said with a firm nod. "I'll teach you what I know."

I sighed with relief. What I'd told him was true. I didn't want to be the only one on the ship who couldn't defend herself. If I was going to be living among the Vandar raiders for the foreseeable future, I might as well learn to fight like them. I'd despised how powerless I'd felt when the ship had been attacked and my only option had been to hide.

I knew that the Raas would do everything he could to protect me, but I also knew that he couldn't always be with me. And at the present moment, he clearly wanted to be anywhere *but* near me.

"Can we start now?" I asked, gathering my skirts up to leave.

Krin eyed me. "You can't fight in that."

I glanced down at the loose fabric that covered me all the way down to my toes. He was right. I could barely move in the voluminous dress, much less fight in it. I knew the Raas had disposed of my old clothes, and there was nothing in the cabinets but more dresses like the one I wore and short nightgowns. "I don't have anything else."

Krin thought for a moment, looking me up and down, then grinned. "I've got an idea. *Vaes.*"

CHAPTER
TWENTY-FOUR

Kratos

I stood at the illuminated star chart in my strategy room, peering at the colored dots moving across the glass. We were no closer to finding the Zagrath who ordered the attack on my ship than we were when we started, but I'd spent considerably more time staring at the map than I ever had before. Part of that was my determination to hunt down the enemy that dared order an invasion of my ship, and part was because I could not return to my quarters. At least not when Astrid was awake.

Her observations had unnerved me and made me doubt my mission for the first time in my life. I knew that a Raas could not doubt. Doubt was weakness, and weakness led to defeat and death. No, there was no room in my head for her insights. Not if I wished to remain strong. And remain the Raas.

As much as I feared that she would weaken me, I could not stay away from her altogether. At night, I took her with an abandon I could not during the day. In the dark, I poured all my desires and needs into her, memorizing her body with my fingers, my tongue, and my tail, savoring her cries and moans. I fucked her until I was sated, and she was trembling from her release. Each night, we fell asleep with our slick bodies entwined, and those moments carried me through the long days. But still, I missed the soft lilt of her humming, the pretty flush on her cheeks when I disrobed, and the hungry look in her green eyes just before I buried my cock in her.

A pounding on the door made me banish my thoughts of her and press my hard cock down with my arms folded in front of me. "*Vaes.*"

Bron strode inside when the doors slid open, his eyes going to me then to the star chart. "I thought I might find you here."

"Where are they?" I asked, gesturing to the clear chart that took up most of one wall.

"No doubt hiding like the cowards they are."

I grunted and turned back to the chart, tapping my finger on a distant planet. "We've tracked ships on a trajectory to this planet lately. Maybe this is the new Zagrath outpost. It's outside the neutral zone, but not close to Vandar space."

Bron stepped closer. "That would be a smart move for the Zagrath. It's close enough to their territory that they could easily defend it."

"Yet they don't," I said. "Sensors have picked up no blockades or regular patrols."

"Then maybe it isn't a new outpost. The Zagrath rarely set up a military outpost without fortifying it."

I tapped the glass. "Which tips us off. What if they're

leaving this outpost undefended so we don't identify it as military?"

Bron nodded. "That would be clever. Risky, but clever."

"It is what we would do."

"True, but the Zagrath rarely do what we would do."

"Until now," I said, my certainty growing. I dragged both hands through my hair. "Set a course for this planet."

Bron clicked his heels. "Yes, Raas." He turned to go, then hesitated. "Do you mind if I ask if everything is okay, Raas?"

I flinched. "Why?"

"You look like you are not sleeping, Kratos. And you never leave the command deck."

His use of my name meant he was talking to me as my friend. It was true I wasn't sleeping much, but that was because I was up half the night fucking the female who captivated my every waking moment—trying desperately to burn off my obsession with her. It was not because I was working.

"I thought you told me I needed to be seen on the command deck more," I said, my voice sharp. "Well, here I am."

My *majak* frowned at me. "I did not mean that you should abandon everything for command, Raas."

"That is what it is to be Raas."

He drew in a long breath before continuing. "I know you do not see her anymore, Raas. I know she spends her days with the boy. I know she eats her meal with him every night."

Of course, my *majak* would know these things. He had assigned the apprentice. He would get reports from the boy. He probably knew more about her than I did. I remembered what Astrid had told me about Bron, and knew she was right. Bron asked me questions I did not welcome because he was my loyal *majak*.

"What do you know?" I asked, hating the worry in my voice. "Is she unhappy?"

"Do you care?"

I spun away from him in frustration, bracing my arms wide on the ebony desk. "My loyalty is to the Vandar. Not to her happiness."

"Agreed, Raas. But you did take her as your prize. I can only assume you have claimed her. If you do not wish to keep her, you should let her go."

I rounded on him. "I will not give her up!"

His expression did not waver, even as I shook with anger. "So, you *do* care."

I raked both hands through my hair. "I cannot let my need for her weaken me."

I should not have admitted this to anyone, but there was no one I trusted more than Bron.

"Raas." His voice was low. "Desire does not have to weaken you. Are we weaker for visiting pleasure planets?"

"No, but she is not like a pleasurer," I said. "I cannot fuck her and forget about her."

"Then I think I would consider you lucky, Raas."

I choked out a laugh. "I do not feel lucky. I feel like I'm being ripped in two."

"Just because you are passionate about the female does not mean you are any less passionate for your people or your mission." Bron put a hand on my shoulder. "You are a big enough Vandar warrior to contain both, I think."

I met my *majak's* gaze. "You are wise, my friend. My Raisa was right about you."

His eyebrows lifted. "Your Raisa?" His gaze dropped to my markings then back to my eyes. "Raas?"

I shook my head, knowing I'd said too much. "I know it is impossible."

He was silent for a moment. "What was she right about me?"

"She said you want to protect me, and that no one was more loyal to me than you."

The edges of his mouth twitched. "I have always liked that female of yours."

I allowed myself a smile. "Not too much, I hope."

"Not too much," he said. "But since we are talking of her, you should probably know that she is currently in the battle ring."

"What?" I jerked up. "Why is she in the battle ring?"

"The boy is teaching her to fight. At her request."

The thought of Astrid fighting made my blood run hot. It wasn't the fighting I disapproved of. It was that I wasn't the one teaching her. I let out a low growl.

"I assume I have the command deck?" Bron asked.

"You assume correctly," I told him as I stomped out of my strategy room and headed for the battle ring.

I moved quickly through the ship—leaping down entire flights of stairs—with warriors jumping out of my way as I passed. When I reached the cage, though, I did not rush in. I held back and watched as the female and the boy called Krin circled each other, sparring sticks in their hands. Her pale hair was pulled up high on her head, and his tail swished quickly behind him.

I let out a sigh of relief. At least they were not using real weapons. I narrowed my eyes. But what was she wearing? Not the clothes that I'd had brought to her. No, she appeared to have on one of the cloth apprentice kilts, and one of her silky sleeping tops she'd knotted at the waist.

I clenched my fists. Most of her legs were exposed, and her stomach flashed each time she lifted her arms. The soft flesh I kissed and nipped and licked in the dark was now on display for all to see. As my pulse raced, I realized that I missed *seeing* her. Even though I buried my cock in her every night, I missed looking on the creaminess of her skin and the pink flush of her cheeks and the gentle bow of her lips.

Astrid spun and lunged for Krin, her kilt flying up and exposing the curve of one ass cheek. I almost groaned out loud as my cock hardened. Watching her in the battle cage was more arousing than I would have imagined, even with my female in her ridiculous makeshift outfit. Her face was flushed with exertion and her eyes glittered in concentration.

Once again, I saw the flash of steely determination that had drawn me to her. The strength that would make her a great Raisa. If only...

Enough, I thought. I had stayed away from her for too long.

I climbed the steps and threw open the cage door, causing both Astrid and Krin to pivot to face me. "If you wanted to learn, you should have asked."

CHAPTER

TWENTY-FIVE

Astrid

I stared at him, almost dropping the sparring stick. It had been days since I'd actually seen the Raas, and I'd almost forgotten how huge and imposing he was. As he stood with his legs set wide, his back muscles were flared out from his corded stomach and his arms were like veined granite. I drew up the courage to look at his face and was almost breathless when I saw his sharp cheekbones and dark flashing eyes.

Krin quickly tapped his heels together, throwing his chest back as Kratos entered the ring.

"You can go." The Raas nodded to him. "I'll teach the female."

I bristled at his words and at the assumption that I wanted him to teach me. "I didn't ask you to teach me to fight. I asked Krin."

Krin had handed him his sparring rod and was backing toward the door. When I said this, he froze.

Raas narrowed his eyes at me. "You would rather this apprentice teach you than the Raas?"

"At least he's been around," I shot back, watching his eyes narrow.

"I have been around," he said. "Have you not enjoyed my attentions?"

My face warmed as I noticed a few Vandar warriors outside the battle ring. I stepped closer to him, my voice almost a hiss. "I thought I was only for you to screw at night. If that's all you want from me, why are you here?"

A muscle ticked in his jaw. "I'm here to teach you. You want to learn how to fight?"

I nodded, even though I still didn't want him to be the one to teach me.

"Let's see what you've learned so far, human." He inclined his head at me, raising his rod across his chest. "*Vaes.*"

I glared at him, all the fury from the past few days bubbling up in me. With a yell, I ran at him, my sparring rod over my head. I wanted to bring it down on his arm, but instead, Kratos deftly sidestepped me. He spun on his heel and brought his own sparring rod down across my ass then followed that by a sharp swat with his tail.

"Ow!" I leapt away from him, one hand going to my smarting backside.

"Never leave yourself open like that," he said, as he circled me. "And never let anger make you lose your focus."

There were a few muffled laughs from outside the ring. I tried to ignore them, but my cheeks burned with humiliation and my ass stung from the sharp hit. "Asshole."

His brows lifted, but he wasn't angry—only amused,

which made me want to hurt him even more. "Fighting is not the only thing you are learning, I see."

"You've inspired me," I snapped.

I steadied my breath and tried to focus on the few things Krin had told me before Kratos had interrupted. I need to keep my weapon high and move my feet. I saw how Kratos circled me and tried to mimic him in the other direction.

A grin teased the corners of his mouth. "Good, Raisa," he murmured low so only I could hear him. "You move well, but then I already knew that."

Fresh heat scorched my cheeks at the reference to our nights together. But if he thought he was going to rattle me, he was sorely mistaken. "That's the only thing you seem to know about me."

He tilted his head slightly. "Oh, I know everything about you, female. I know how you taste. I know how you sound when I'm moving inside you. I know how you cry out when I suck that sweet little nub of yours."

Warmth pulsed between my legs, and I wished—not for the first time—that the Vandar believed in underwear. I shot daggers at him with my eyes, flicking my gaze quickly outside the ring to see if any of the gathering Vandar could hear him. But they seemed to be more concerned with laughing and talking amongst themselves than listening to what Kratos was saying to me in hushed tones.

"Are you going to attack me again, or just stand there, wishing me dead?" he asked.

Pressing my lips together to keep myself from cursing him again, I dove forward, swinging my rod at his stomach. He blocked my stick with his own, then snatched my sparring rod from my hands and swatted me on the ass with it.

"Stop doing that," I yelled, as I stumbled away from him. My ass burned, but I could also feel the slickness between my thighs. More than I hated Kratos for smacking me, I hated myself for getting aroused by it.

He tossed me my rod. "Stop making it so easy."

I put my hands on my hips. "Are you going to actually teach me something, or just use this as an excuse to spank me?"

He cocked one eyebrow. "You really want to learn to fight like a Vandar?"

I threw my hands up. "That's why I asked Krin to teach me. I don't want to be the only one on board who can't defend herself."

"You're sure you just don't want to learn so you can fight me off?"

Now it was my turn to raise an eyebrow. "You really think I stand a chance against a Raas of the Vandar? I couldn't fight you off even if I wanted to."

He smiled at that. "But you don't want to, do you?"

I didn't, and he knew it.

Without waiting for an answer, he pointed to my feet. "Keep them wide, but keep them moving. Like this." He moved to one side.

I copied him, and he nodded. "Weapon up. Good. Now don't tell me what you're doing before you do it. Come at me without raising your weapon until the last possible moment."

I hesitated, then advanced on him, keeping my rod level until I was almost on him. Then I jabbed it at his leg, making contact.

Leaping back, I raised my arms in the air. "I did it. I got y—!"

Before I could finish my sentence, he'd lunged forward and grabbed me, spinning me and wrapping one arm around my shoulder, then jerking me flush to his huge body, his tail coiling around my legs so I couldn't kick at him. "Never celebrate a victory until your opponent is dead at your feet, Raisa. Now you've just provoked him."

My breathing was heavy as I struggled in his grasp. "Let me go."

"I don't think so," he purred into my ear, the low buzz of his words sending frissons of pleasure down my spine. "Not when you're so eager to punish me."

"You're the one who keeps slapping my ass," I said.

"Only because you insist on flashing it to half my ship." His tail flicked at the hem of my kilt. "What are you wearing, Raisa?"

"The only thing Krin could find for me for sparring." I gripped the thick arm crossing my chest and tugged at it. "The dresses you got for me are impossible to move in."

"They're meant to cover you so no other male can see what I get to see."

"Is it your crew you trust so little, or me?" I said between stolen breaths. "Do you really think I want anyone but you?"

His grip relaxed slightly. "No." His tail slipped down and underneath the hem of the kilt, sliding between my wet thighs. He growled. "I can feel how much you want me. If there were not people watching, I would fuck you right here on this mat."

"That's all you care about, right?" I dug my fingers into his flesh. "You don't want to see me or talk to me. You just want to fuck me in the dark."

It was getting easier and easier to swear at him, although I'd only whispered the word.

"Don't you like it?" His mouth hummed against my throat and my entire body heated. "From the way you scream, I thought you liked to have my cock buried inside you."

I thrashed against him, finally loosening his grip and slipping out from under his arm. "You can't keep screwing my brains out and then leaving me! That's not what I signed up for!"

The sounds of the other warriors vanished. The battle ring was silent and so was everyone watching. The Raas stood across from me, his dark eyes burning into me.

"This is not what you signed up for?" He sounded like he didn't believe what I had said. "You signed up to be mine."

He took a menacing step toward me, and I backed up. In a second, I knew I'd gone too far. I'd yelled at him in front of his crew, and he couldn't let that go. My body shook as he advanced on me. I'd never seen him so enraged, his chest heaving and his neck muscles straining.

"That means you belong to me, in whatever way I want you." He crossed to me in an instant, throwing me over his shoulder and slapping my ass hard. "Now I'm going to remind you exactly what you signed up for, female."

CHAPTER
TWENTY-SIX

Kratos

I pounded down the corridors to my quarters, the female bouncing on my back as I didn't attempt to cushion my footfall. She hadn't made a sound since I'd picked her up, and I had not tried to talk to her. I was too furious. Furious at her for calling me out in front of my crew, but more livid at myself for giving her cause to think I didn't want to be around her.

She'd been right to think that. I had been doing just what she'd accused me of—fucking her in the dark and then leaving before I had to see her or talk to her. But it wasn't entirely her fault. I couldn't avoid her just because she had a talent for seeing into people, and I hadn't liked what she'd seen in me.

I also knew that if I didn't get her out of that battle ring and back to my quarters I would be tempted to spread her legs and fuck her right there on the mat with all the warriors watching. I'd had no idea how arousing it would be to spar with the female, and I did not want to rut like an animal in the middle of the battle ring.

We reached the door to my quarters and I entered, swinging her down from my shoulder and setting her down in front of me. I'd expected her to be subdued after being spanked and then carried across the ship, but she wasn't. Although there were tear streaks down her face, her eyes burned as she looked up at me.

I turned away, not wanting to see the evidence that I'd made her cry, and waved a hand toward the cabinets. "Take off that apprentice kilt. It's not suitable for you to wear."

"I'm not putting on those dresses again."

"Fine," I turned and closed the distance between us in a single long stride. "Wear nothing. I would enjoy you walking around my quarters naked."

"One less thing to bother with when you sneak into bed at night, right?" Her words were sharp, but her voice shook.

"You think I only want you at night, Raisa?" I growled, taking her jaw in one hand. "I think about you all day every day until I think I might go mad from my desire for you. Only when I can't take being away from you for another moment do I come to bed and bury myself in you."

Her mouth opened but no words came out of her mouth.

"It is not that I don't want you," I husked. "It is that I want you too much. I'm afraid if I don't leave you, I'll lose myself in you—I'll lose myself in us."

For several moments, we stood glaring at each other and heaving in breaths. Then, without looking away from me, she shimmied the kilt down over her hips until it dropped to the floor, then she pulled the top over her head. When she stood in front of me with nothing on, she gave me a shy smile. "I wouldn't mind getting lost with you, Raas."

Tvek. The tip of my tail twitched, and my cock hardened. It was impossible to maintain my anger when she was offering herself to me so openly. Scooping her up, I carried her to the bed and lay her down, taking a moment to appreciate her lying completely naked, her light hair fanned out behind her head on the black sheets. She was all curves and softness, and she was mine.

Her eyes were half-lidded with desire, her pupils dark and large. She licked her lower lip as she watched me take off my kilt and belt and drop them to the floor.

It took every bit of self-restraint I had not to spread her legs and plunge myself into her, but I wanted this to be slow. I wanted to show her I wasn't always a brute who took what he wanted.

I brushed my lips over hers, my tongue teasing her seam. She let out a breathy sound and I parted her lips, letting my tongue caress hers slowly. She'd moved her hands from my shoulders to my chest and her fingers were bumping across the ridges of my stomach. I tore my mouth from hers, knowing where her hands were going.

"Not yet, Raisa. Not until I've gotten my fill of you."

I kissed my way down her throat to her breasts, licking the pebbled flesh around her nipples one at a time and finally sucking on the hard peaks. She tangled her fingers in my hair and moaned when I continued to trace my tongue down the soft swell of her belly until I'd reached her sex.

"Kratos," she said, her wispy words more a plea than anything.

"Soon," I told her, spreading her legs and finding the little nub that made her go so wild. I began to swirl my tongue over it, slipping one thick finger inside her while she writhed. I sucked her slick nub while dragging my finger in and out slowly, until my female's cries were piercing, and her body convulsed around my finger.

Sliding it out of her, I put my finger in my mouth and sucked down all of her sweetness. She lay with her legs sprawled, her breath shallow. As I looked down at her, I dragged my tail through her slickness, letting the sensitive tip savor her soft skin. Her gaze grew molten as she watched me.

"You like my tail?" I asked.

She nodded, biting on her lower lip. "I like having your tail and your cock at the same time."

"Then I will give you both." I flicked the furry tip over her nub, her gaze darkening with desire.

Picking her up again, I sat on the edge of the bed and set her on my lap so that she straddled me.

Her eyes locked onto mine as I lifted her, notching the crown of my cock at her entrance, her juices already wetting it. She clasped her hands on my shoulders as she slowly lowered herself, taking every bit of my cock. When I'd bottomed out inside her, she rolled her head back.

Threading my hand in her hair, I pulled her face back to me. "Eyes on me, Raisa."

She nodded, her green eyes holding mine as she began to ride.

The feeling of her tight heat sheathing me was incredible, but even better was watching her face as she took me, her pupils widening and her lips parting as she let out breathy gasps each time I thrusted up.

As promised, I wrapped my tail around her, finding her bundle of nerves and working it with the tip. Soon, she was moving fast, her expression wild. Her eyes fluttered shut for a moment.

"Eyes open," I ordered. "Don't look away from me."

"I'm so close, Raas," she panted, locking her gaze on me as her hands slipped on my slick shoulders.

"Your perfect little cunt is trembling," I whispered, wrapping my arms around her back to keep her from falling. I moved my tail faster. "Come for me, Raisa."

She arched her back as her body detonated for a second time, clamping tight around my cock. The vise-like grip and the sensation of my tail between her folds sent me over the edge, and I thrust up hard once more before shooting into her, my own roar mixed with her screams and both echoing through the room. After a moment, I held her face to mine, kissing her even as we both fought for breath.

Flopping back on the bed, I tucked her into my side like I usually did. But instead of it being the dead of night, I could look down onto her light hair and see her small hand splayed across my chest.

"I'm sorry," she said, as she traced a finger over my markings.

"Sorry?" I lifted my head slightly to look at her face. "You do not have to apologize after *that*. Or have you committed some heinous offense I am not aware of?"

She rested her chin on my chest. "I upset you when I talked about your crew."

I smoothed some damp tendrils of hair off her forehead. I should not have been surprised that she'd sensed my feelings. "I was wrong to react the way I did. But you are right that I did not like it, even though you spoke the truth."

One of her eyebrows quirked up. "You think I was right?"

"You see much for a human," I admitted. "I have been wrong to keep you at arm's length."

"I only wanted to help."

165

I pulled her closer to me. "I am not used to being given things freely. Always, I have had to take by force."

"Technically, you did take me by force," she said, her tone teasing.

I slapped her bare ass. "I took nothing you did not want to give, Raisa."

She yelped. "Again with the spanking?"

I laughed. "You seem to enjoy provoking me."

"Not as much as you enjoy smacking my ass."

I rubbed her soft flesh where I'd slapped her. "Your gift of perception is more impressive than I thought."

She wiggled in my grasp. "Very funny."

I moved my hand from her ass and pulled her so that she was completely on top of me. "I will not spank you anymore if you will tell me more of what you see."

She stilled. "What I see?"

"You were right about my *majak* and my war chief, and you barely spent any time with them. I would like to know what you think about the rest of my crew."

She hesitated. "You are sure? You won't get angry and disappear again?"

I held her green eyes with my own solemn gaze and saw the pain in their depths. Pain I had caused. "I will never leave you again, Raisa. That is a promise from your Raas."

Something softened in her expression, and she drew in a long breath, finally nodding. "As long as you're sure."

As she launched into her thoughts on my crew, her soft voice eagerly rising and falling, I knew I'd never been more sure about anything.

CHAPTER
TWENTY-SEVEN

Astrid

I don't know why I decided to trust Kratos. It didn't make sense. He was a warlord of the Vandar who had taken me from my sister and seduced me like a spider luring a fly into a web. He was Raas Kratos, known for raining destruction on the Zagrath Empire and terrorizing anyone who stood with them. He was huge and powerful and used to being obeyed. But he also looked at me like no one ever had before—as if I was valuable and rare and to be cherished. I'd never seen that look directed at me before. It was intoxicating and filled me with a strange sense of power.

But I'd seen something else in his eyes—a deep-held pain I recognized all too well—that made me believe him when he promised not to leave me again. He knew what it was to be alone, and he hated it as much as I did.

"You must go?" I asked, fastening his shoulder armor

across his chest, my fingers feathering along his bare skin as they expertly worked the leather strap. I'd become used to dressing and undressing him, and I now looked forward to touching him freely, as I stripped away the trappings of war.

He made a noise in the back of his throat that told me he was not eager to leave me, either. "My warriors have received a distress call from a colony the Zagrath are attempting to subjugate. We must take a short detour from our mission and respond."

"You get distress calls?" Even though he'd told me all the ways the Vandar hordes protected others from the choking control of the insidious empire, I was still adjusting my mind from what I'd always been told. It was a different story than the one the Zagrath spread.

He shifted from one foot to the other, watching me as I tightened the metal shoulder cap. "To races who do not wish to be ruled by the empire and pay taxes for the honor of being controlled by fleets of faceless soldiers, the Vandar are saviors."

"I'm sure Corvak is pleased at the chance to engage in battle."

A slow grin crossed his face. "No doubt. But, as you suggested, I gave him more responsibility, and he has repaid that with a renewed loyalty."

My hands lingered on the hard planes of his chest. "Good. I believe he would be a dangerous foe. You should always keep him close."

He looped an arm around my waist and pulled me to him. "If my warriors knew I was being counseled by a human female, they would think I was crazy."

His heart thumped heavily and reverberated through my own chest, sending frissons of pleasure across my skin. "It will be our secret, Raas."

Lowering his head so that his long hair fell forward and brushed my cheeks, he inhaled deeply. "I like having secrets with you. I never imagined a human would become the most valuable member of my crew."

"Aside from your *majak*." I'd seen how close he and Bron were, and I did not presume to hold a position as valuable as that.

His hand slipped down and squeezed my ass. "There are some things even a *majak* cannot do for me. Things that you do very well."

My face warmed, pleased that the Raas enjoyed our nights tangled around each other, my moans and cries mingling with his deeper, dominant sounds. I slapped his chest playfully then caught the tip of his tail as he wound it around my waist. "You should stop before you make it necessary for me to undress you again."

He growled and the noise tickled my ear and sent a jolt down my spine. "I would not mind that, Raisa." Then he gave a pointed look at his tail. "And you should stop stroking my tail if you truly do not wish to detain me."

I pulled back, dropped his tail, and peered up at him, my face warming. "I forget that touching your tail is a turn on. You should attend to the distress call."

His dark eyes closed for a moment, and he released a breath. "For someone who thought we were brutal beasts not long ago, you have become my greatest taskmaster."

"If you tell me you want to save people from the Zagrath, I will believe you." I met his gaze when he looked at me again. "You have never lied to me."

He took my hand in his and raised it to his lips, kissing my open palm slowly. "And you have never given me unwise counsel."

His lips seared my skin, making my pulse skitter wildly. I

169

pushed him away with my other hand. "You should go before I change my mind and decide that the distress call can wait."

Laughing low, he swept me up in a hard kiss, releasing me quickly and backing away. With a final scorching gaze, he spun on his heel, his battle kilt slapping his thighs as he left.

I had only a moment to catch my breath before Krin was entering the room, his face flushed. I'd grown used to the sight of the boy's excitement when there was even the slightest possibility that the Vandar horde would engage in battle. The fact that he thrilled at warfare didn't quell my nerves, though.

"What happens when the Vandar respond to a distress call?" I asked after the boy had wolfed down one of the knots of bread I'd saved for him.

He shrugged. "Depends."

I swept up handfuls of my skirt as I joined him at the table. "On?"

He swallowed another bite of bread. "A lot of things— how many Zagrath fighters have been left behind, if there is a full garrison, how many of the residents are armed and willing to join in the battle."

"Do the Vandar always win?"

Krin dragged a hand through his messy hair and gave me a lopsided grin. "Of course." Then he frowned. "That doesn't mean the Zagrath don't come back or send more soldiers. Sometimes the colony is too important or the resources too valuable or the location too strategic."

"And the Vandar never leave warriors behind?"

He wrinkled his nose. "We are a horde. We are always on the move and cannot be locked to one place."

I remembered what the Raas had told me about his people. They'd always been nomadic, and it was a tradition they'd maintained when they'd taken to space. It had probably kept them from being decimated by their enemy, but it also meant they constantly put out fires that could be started again. It was no wonder the Vandar and Zagrath had been locked in a cat and mouse battle for generations. It was also easy to understand how the Zagrath had been able to create the image of the Vandar as indiscriminate brutes instead of freedom fighters.

The sound of pounding footsteps echoed outside the door, and Krin eyed it longingly.

"Warriors heading for transports?" I asked.

He nodded. "They're going down to the planet."

I angled my head at him. "Why don't we go?"

He was already shaking his head before the words had left my mouth. "To the planet?"

"No. To watch the warriors depart for battle. I'm sure the Raas wouldn't mind if we stayed out of the way."

Krin bit the corner of his lip. "I don't know. It didn't go so well the last time you talked me into something."

"I told you. The Raas didn't punish me for wanting to learn how to fight. And I did learn how to defend myself. I may not be able to hold off a Vandar warrior—or an apprentice—but I'll be ready if mercenaries ever board the ship again."

Krin stuck out his chest. "If that happens, I'll help you fight them off."

"See? That's why the Raas assigned you to me. He won't mind if we watch warriors depart for battle together."

The boy seemed to debate within himself for a moment before finally nodding. "Okay, but we'll have to make sure the Raas doesn't see us. Or the battle chief."

"Agreed." Even though I'd advised Raas Kratos about handling Corvak, I knew the Vandar warrior did not approve of my presence. The less he was reminded of me, the better.

Krin led the way out to the corridor and talked briefly to the guard, who darted a disapproving glance at me before giving a curt nod. The huge Vandar strode off down first one curving staircase and then another, as Krin as I hurried behind him.

When it seemed like we'd descended into the bowels of the ship and it couldn't possibly go down any further, we stepped through wide doors and were inside a cavernous hangar bay. The same enormous space where I'd first arrived.

Menacing Vandar warriors rushed by us toward transport ships, their boots pounding the iron floor. Their bellows were drowned out by the sound of roaring engines as ship after ship tore across the hangar bay floor and shot into space through the open mouth at the far end.

Krin jerked me out of the way and back against the wall. My heart raced as warriors ran eagerly onto vessels, snatches of the battle cry "For Vandar!" floating on the air.

My gaze was pulled to a larger ship loaded full of warriors. Raas Kratos stood flanked by his *majak* and his battle chief as the ramp lifted. He saw me, but his body betrayed nothing. He did not flinch even as his dark, blazing eyes never left mine.

The Raas was going into battle, and as his ship rocketed across the hangar bay, I felt like a part of my soul was going with him.

CHAPTER
TWENTY-EIGHT

Kratos

I t had been all I could do not to storm off the transport and drag her back to my quarters. Even though I had given Astrid the freedom to move throughout the ship, the sight of her watching me go into battle was unsettling. I did not want my pretty, soft female anywhere near the brutality of battle. I did not want her to see what I had to do to protect the galaxy or what it took for me to be Raas.

It was one thing for her to advise me. It was another for her to be witness to my command.

My muscles ached as I entered my quarters, and I paused as my eyes adjusted to the dark. The battle had been successful, and we had repelled the Zagrath with no casualties in the colony, but we had lost two of our Vandar warriors in the fighting. I knew they were being welcomed into Zedna as conquering heroes by Lokken and all of the ancient gods and ancestors, but my heart was still heavy.

I'd returned to the command deck after the battle, locking in our course to the planet I still wished to investigate before leaving my *majak* in command. Even though my battle chief had looked at me askance as I'd strode off to my quarters, I needed to check on Astrid before I could focus on our mission again. I needed to know she was safe, and see her with my own eyes.

Once I'd acclimated to the dimness, I could make out the glint of iron above my bed and hear her breathing gently below the welded shields and axes. I unhooked my armor and hung it on the stand next to the door, then tugged off my boots and stepped out of my battle kilt, leaving them all in a heap. I glanced at the small figure in my huge bed. I wanted nothing more than to collapse beside Astrid, but the sweat and blood from the battle lingered on my flesh.

Padding into the bathing chamber, I flicked on soft lights and lowered my body into the steaming crimson water long enough for the remnants of the battle to melt away, along with the knots in my muscles. I did not linger long, stepping out and shaking droplets of water off me before squeezing the wet tip of my tail. I didn't bother to stand over the loud drying vents, instead making my way as quietly as possible to the bed—lit now by faint light spilling from the bathing chamber—and slipping beneath the sheets.

As if pulled by some gravitational force, Astrid rolled over in her sleep and draped one arm across my chest, sighing softly. Even though I wanted to flip her on her back and bury my cock inside her, I did not. I had stopped waking her like that, preferring to see her eyes on me as I claimed her.

I did stroke my hand down her slender arm, her warmth

stilling my breath and forcing thoughts of the battle from my mind. Her presence had become a steadying force—an anchor in the storm—and one I could not imagine being without.

"You're back."

I glanced down and saw that she'd woken. "Shhhhh. Go back to sleep, Raisa."

She lifted her head to meet my eyes. "Are you okay?" She moved her hand over my chest. "You weren't hurt?"

"I was not hurt."

She let out a breath, sinking back down. "I tried to wait up for you, but I got sleepy."

"You should sleep," I said, pulling her so her body was flush against mine.

"You're sure?" Her voice held a hint of teasing.

"I am sure." As much as I loved the feel of being inside her, I wanted to stay like we were, our bodies rising and falling as we breathed together.

"Were you...?" she started to say. "How was the battle?"

"We were victorious. The Zagrath fled like scuttling insects, and the colony is free to rule itself again."

"I'm glad."

I held her arm to me. "Are you? You no longer think the Vandar are brutes and me the worst of them?"

"I know you're not. I've seen the good in you and in your warriors."

Hearing the words from her lips made my chest swell. It should not matter to me, a Raas of the Vandar, what a human female thought. But it did.

She traced one finger over my markings as neither of us spoke for a few beats. "Tell me about these. The Vandar all have tattoos on their chests, but they're all a bit different."

"You wish to talk about my markings?" I asked, amused

that she was changing the subject. "Now?"

"You've never explained them to me before. Do they mean rank or status?"

"They are not tattoos. We are born with them."

She sat up halfway to take in the black swirls that curled up and over my shoulders. "I'd thought that might be rumor. Do all Vandar have them?"

"Only the males," I told her. "And the females once they've sealed the mating bond."

"What does that mean?" Her fingers feathered over my damp skin and made me shiver.

"When a Vandar female mates with the male she is supposed to be with for life, his marks appear on her, as well. And his marks extend to cover more of his chest and arms."

Her eyebrows popped up. "So if the marks never appear..."

"Then the couple is not fated to be."

"But what if you fall for someone and the marks don't appear?"

My throat tightened. "A Vandar can only impregnate a female with his marks."

A look of understanding crossed her face. "So if you aren't fated, then you can never have children."

"And you are meant to be with another."

She cocked her head at me. "So you have to screw a bunch of Vandar women to find your match?"

I couldn't help the laugh that escaped my lips. "It does not usually take so long, but the Vandar do not believe in monogamy until you find your mate."

"And then?"

I frowned at her. "You ask a lot of questions."

She shrugged. "Since I'm living on a raider ship now, I probably should." Her fingers stilled on my skin. "Do non-Vandar females ever get the marks on them?"

I'd wondered how long it would take her to think of this. I did not want to tell her, but I could not lie. "I have never heard of it happening, but Vandar do not usually intermingle with other species for any significant amount of time."

"I'm guessing a pleasurer has never gotten marks after a wild night?"

I shook my head. "A Vandar raider's one true mate would not be an alien pleasurer."

Astrid sat up all the way, her eyes not leaving my marks. "I guess a human probably wouldn't be, either."

"I do not know," I admitted.

"So, you took me captive and claimed me and told me I was yours but that's not really true, is it?" Her voice was almost a whisper. "I'm just something for you to amuse yourself with before you find the right Vandar female."

"You are not amusement for me. You know that." I sat up and wrapped my arms around her back. "You are my Raisa."

She shook her head. "I don't understand what that means."

"I was not completely honest with you before," I said. "Raisa does not mean lady. It means queen. A Raas's queen."

"I can't be your queen if you need to ditch me someday."

I tried to swallow, but my throat was too thick. Everything she said was true. Without mating marks, there was no future for us. As perfect as she felt for me, the human could not be mine forever. Not unless I wanted to defy the traditions of my people.

I stroked her pale, unmarked skin. "You will always be my Raisa." I wanted to tell her more to assure her—to explain that I didn't care about marks or fate or even children if it meant losing her—but the ship shuddered and a siren began to wail.

TWENTY-NINE

Kratos

"Report," I said as I walked onto the command deck, my voice booming. My crew to jerked to attention, clicking their heels.

Bron looked up from his standing console, wrinkles creasing his forehead. "We've reached the planet you wanted to investigate, Raas. It was not far from the colony we assisted."

I focused my gaze out the wide viewing screen. The small, blue planet lay ahead, along with what looked to be a fleet of gunmetal-gray Zagrath ships massed between us and the surface. I knew my own horde of warbirds was flanked behind my lead ship, and from the faint purple glow of the command deck, I could tell we'd activated our invisibility shielding.

"It was a trap," Corvak said, his voice dark and deadly as

he approached me. "This pointless search has led us straight into a Zagrath snare."

"What happened?" I asked.

"As you ordered, once we left the colony, we resumed our course. When we reached the planet, we activated our sensors."

I knew our sensors would alert ships to our presence even if we were hidden from view. "And you located the fleet?"

"Not until they appeared from behind the planet."

So, Corvak was right. They had been waiting for us. The planet had been a lure, and they had flown ships to it with enough regularity that we would suspect it to be of importance.

I let a low rumble escape my lips. "Damage?"

"Minimal," my battle chief said, his voice now steady. "But they know we're here. Would you like to call the attack, Raas?"

I rocked back on my heels, appraising the Zagrath fleet and wondering how many more were behind the planet, waiting to emerge. I was used to taking my enemy unaware. I did not like to have the element of surprise used against me.

"Raas," one of my warriors said, turning from his standing post to face me and clicking his heels together. "There is an incoming hail."

"From one of our ships?" I asked.

He shook his head. "From the Zagrath."

This was new. The empire rarely deigned to acknowledge our existence, considering us more of an irritation to be ignored than an enemy to be negotiated with. To communicate with us would be to acknowledge that we were a viable threat and a formidable foe.

"Should I put it through to your strategy room?"

I felt the eyes on me. "No." I inclined my head to the wide screen. "Put it through here. Let them see our warriors preparing to destroy them."

Corvak grunted in approval next to me, pivoting to face the screen and holding his battle axe in front of him. Bron also came to stand on my other side, crossing his arms tightly over his chest. I set my feet wide, bracing my own hands on my hips with my biceps flexed. I knew we made a menacing trio. Exactly what I wanted the Zagrath to see.

The screen flickered, the view of the enemy fleet replaced by the view of a well-lit command deck and a single Zagrath officer in a smoke-blue uniform. Other Zagrath were in the background, sitting at gleaming-white consoles, their eyes fixed on us.

"I am Commander Quijon of the Zagrath Empire," the Zagrath officer said, his hands clasped behind his back. "To whom am I speaking?"

This Zagrath was everything I was not, with his close-cropped, fair hair and crisp uniform. I narrowed my eyes at him, hating everything he stood for and everything his empire had done. "Raas Kratos of the Vandar."

The commander cleared his throat. "As you can see, your ships are outnumbered and outgunned. At least, they will be shortly, once our second fleet arrives."

I did not respond. I only glared at the screen, although I felt Corvak shift by my side. I suspected the thought of being flanked in the rear by the Zagrath did not sit well with him.

"We do not wish a battle today," the Zagrath commander continued. "We only wish you to return what you took from an imperial ship."

I tried to keep from flinching, but I could not prevent the sneer that curled my upper lip. "What do you think the empire has that I want?"

The man let out an impatient breath. "You took a woman off a ship transporting Zagrath supplies, which makes it a Zagrath ship, and I am to understand that she is living on board your ship as a prisoner."

"There is no one on my ship who has not agreed to be here."

The commander took a step closer. "Look, Vandar. I know you used threats to get this girl to come with you. Release her back to us, and none of your crew need to die."

I snorted a laugh. "You think *my* warriors are the ones who will die?"

He flinched noticeably, readjusting his clasped hands. "You will not be so sure once our other ships arrive. I am giving you a chance to give up the girl and go, before we're forced to board your ship and take her from you."

A dark murmur passed through my command deck, and my warriors tensed at the threat. Even Corvak emitted a low rumble and shifted his grip on his battle axe. He might disagree with my actions of late, but no Vandar took threats to their ships lightly. Especially not from a Zagrath in a uniform that had never seen battle.

"You can try," I growled, giving the enemy a menacing smile.

The commander frowned. This was clearly not going like he'd intended. He turned and walked back to a large captain's chair and sat down in it, stretching his arms to the tips of the armrests. "You refuse to surrender your captive?"

"She is not a captive," I said, my heart beating faster as I thought about Astrid. "But I do refuse to surrender her. She belongs to the Vandar now. She came with me of her own free will and agreed to be mine if I let her ship go. I upheld my end of the bargain. Now she is fulfilling hers."

"You can't fly around the empire, raiding ships and taking

our women to be your whores," the commander spat out, his placid face reddening.

I felt Bron's gaze flick to me for a moment. "She is not my whore. But the Vandar can and will continue to raid your ships until you cease trying to bend the galaxy to your will."

The enemy commander pounded a fist onto his chair's armrest. "The Zagrath Empire controls this sector. That is not up for your input, Vandar."

"My name is not Vandar." I took a step forward, my voice low. "I have told you. I am Raas Kratos of the Vandar. Or in your language, the warlord Kratos of the Vandar. I am the son of Raas Bardon of the Vandar and brother to Raas Kaalek and Raas Tor. I do not take orders from a Zagrath, and I will not return the female to you. She is the property of the Vandar, and you will have to go through me to get her."

Corvak pounded the end of his battle axe on the floor, the sound booming through the command deck and even causing the Zagrath commander to jump.

"Have it your way, Vandar." The Zagrath sneered at me, shaking his head. "Prepare for battle." His face vanished and the screen returned to the view of the enemy fleet.

Blood roared in my ears, as I watched the Zagrath ships light up their weapons systems. "I always do."

CHAPTER
THIRTY

Astrid

I clutched the side of the bed as the ship rocked again. After Kratos had thrown on his clothes and run from the room, the firing had paused for a merciful lull, but it had quickly resumed. As I glanced around the room that was pitching back and forth, I understood why the space was so spartan, and why the few pieces of furniture were bolted to the floor. At least nothing was sliding across the floor as we were being attacked.

I still didn't know what exactly was going on, but I guessed it was the Zagrath. They were the only ones brave enough to engage a Vandar horde in battle. Even though the far glass wall looked out onto space, I could see little but flashes of laser fire and gray-hulled ships in the distance.

I braced my feet on the floor to keep from slipping. I'd heard about the fights between the Zagrath battleships and the Vandar warbirds, the skies filled with explosions and laser fire. I'd never imagined I'd be in one.

Over the wailing sirens and the incoming weapons fire, I heard a thumping on the door. I managed to pull on a dress and made my way to the door by walking with my arms outstretched for balance. I pressed the panel to the side, sending the doors gliding open. Krin hurried in. The guard outside glanced back at me, then resumed staring straight ahead. I guessed even with a battle raging, Kratos had told him to stay put.

"What are you doing here?" I asked Krin, although I was happier to see him than I wanted to let on.

"I know the last battle wasn't fun for you, so I thought I'd make sure you were okay."

I was touched that the boy had been worried for me. "The *majak* didn't send you?"

He shook his head. "He didn't have to send me. I know the Raas would want me to make sure you aren't scared. He seems to like you an awful lot. I've never seen him look at any of the ladies in the fancy houses like he looks at you." He blushed as soon as he said this, dropping his gaze to the floor.

"It's okay," I told him, swaying slightly as the ship shuddered. "I know he's gone to pleasure houses, but I'm glad to know he likes me more than the ladies there." I pulled him into a quick hug, ruffling his hair. "Thanks for that, and thanks for checking on me."

When I let him go, his cheeks were splotched with pink, and I could tell he was attempting to look like he hadn't enjoyed the hug, tugging at his kilt as his tail swished.

"Do you know what's going on?" I asked him, waving a hand to the door. "I can't leave this room."

He cleared his throat and straightened his shoulders,

clearly feeling important getting to impart the information to me. "We shouldn't leave. The Zagrath are attacking, and everyone's busy preparing for a battle on the ship."

"Why would there be a battle on the ship?" I glanced at the wide glass and the laser fire crisscrossing the black sky. "I thought space battles were fought in, well, space."

Krin smiled at me like I was the child and he was the grownup. "The fastest way to bring a battle to an end is to board a ship and take it."

The Vandar were called raiders for a reason. They almost always boarded ships, stripping them of anything valuable before destroying them.

"So, the Vandar are getting ready to board some Zagrath ships?"

The boy nodded, his eyes going to my door. "I saw a bunch of warriors getting on a boarding vessel. If they can take the lead Zagrath ship, we win."

That seemed a little simplistic to me, but then again, I wasn't well-versed in space warfare. "What about Kratos? Is he going with one of the boarding parties?"

Krin's gaze darted to mine then away. "Not this time, at least from what I can see. He's leading the fight from the command deck."

I felt a rush of relief that he wouldn't be leaving the ship and risking his life to board a Zagrath battleship. I knew he was a seasoned fighter, but I hated the thought of him being injured and me not being able to get to him. It was a strange sensation, and one I couldn't completely explain.

"How long do these battles last?" I asked, as another hit made us both stagger to one side.

"Depends," he yelled over the noise. "We don't usually fight so large a fleet."

My heart stuttered slightly. Was there chance the

Vandar would be defeated, or the ship blown up? I didn't like the thought of either option, but I wondered what would happen to me if the ship was taken by the Zagrath. Were they really trying to kill me, or would they consider me a prisoner they were liberating? Regardless, if the Vandar lost, I wouldn't be staying with Kratos. If he even survived.

A hard pit formed in my stomach. I wasn't sure when it had happened, but I'd gone from hoping with all my heart to be rescued to wanting nothing more than to stay with the Vandar warlord who'd taken me as his captive. I'd grown to welcome his hard body moving on top of mine and his deep, claiming kisses. And being desired by him had given me a confidence I hadn't known before. Lying next to him and advising him on his crew and his strategy, I finally felt like I was somewhere I belonged.

Something hard hit the ship, sending both Krin and me to the floor. I caught myself with my hands but as I lay on the cool floor, they stung from the impact. I raised my head to see the boy sprawled close to me.

"Are you okay?"

He looked up and moaned. "I think we're being boarded."

"What?" I pushed myself to standing, and then pulled him up beside me. "Are you sure?"

He rubbed his shoulder where it must have hit the floor. "It felt like a ship clamping on to us."

That wasn't good. I'd already dealt with one boarding party. I did not want to do it again. "Okay, what should we do? If they're coming for me, I need to get the hell out of this room. The last group that came on board looking for me seemed to know where to find me."

Krin's small brow crinkled. "We still have a guard outside."

I'd almost forgotten the hulking Vandar warrior armed to the teeth and standing right outside the door. "Right."

I walked to the door and pressed the panel again, wanting to see the guy and reassure myself that he hadn't run off to take part in the battle. When the doors swished open, I was staring at empty space where the warrior had been. Then my gaze dropped to the floor, and the huge Vandar lying dead in front of the door.

CHAPTER
THIRTY-ONE

Astrid

"Is he...?" I stared down at the guard as blood oozed from his chest.

Krin grabbed my hand and jerked me forward as a blast hit the wall where my head had just been. "*Vaes!*"

I ducked as I scooped up my skirts and ran behind him, the sound of blasters firing behind us. Were they really trying to kill me, or were they just shooting at anything that moved?

We rounded a sharp corner and ran straight into a Zagrath soldier. I'd never seen one so up close and personal. They were tall, and their uniforms were a steely blue, with chest armor of the same color that made them appear wider. Black helmets covered their heads with an eyepiece that snapped down over one eye, making them look a little like automatons.

Even though the Zagrath soldier held a massive laser rifle, Krin didn't hesitate to whip his blade off his belt and jab it up and into the enemy's neck. Blood spurted out, making me stagger back to avoid getting splattered, but Krin grabbed my hand again and pulled me forward.

"We've got to keep moving," he said, holding his dripping knife out as he ran.

I was stunned he'd been able to kill so easily, and wondered if this was the first kill he'd made, or if this was par for the course for Vandar raider apprentices.

"Where are we going?" I asked, after we'd made several more turns.

He paused, looking back at me. "I don't know. Just away from the fighting."

That sounded good to me. The sound of screaming and blaster fire echoed throughout the ship, making my blood run cold. I didn't know how many Zagrath were on board, but it sounded like they were everywhere.

"Wait," I said, pulling my hand from his and stopping. I snatched his blade from him. "I need to do something."

Grabbing the bottom of my dress, I slashed at the fabric until I'd removed everything below my knee. Then I handed him back his blade. "That's better. Now I can actually run without falling."

Krin frowned at my legs, bare from the knee down. "The Raas is not going to like this."

"The Raas isn't here. Would you rather stay alive, or have to run slow to keep up with me and my stupid, long dress?"

"Stay alive."

"Me, too." I took his hand again. "Lead the way."

We hurried down a winding flight of stairs and past the battle ring. Krin jumped over a pair of dead Vandar raiders, but I stumbled when I saw them lying on the floor. I didn't recognize them, but they were muscular and dark-haired—like all Vandar—and made me think of Kratos. What would I do if I saw his body, lifeless on the floor?

I shook my head hard, forcing the thought out of my head and trying not to dwell on just how heartbroken I knew I'd be.

He's fine, I told myself. *He's not dead. He's definitely not dead.*

Krin tugged at my hand but his voice wasn't harsh. "Are you okay?"

I nodded, looking away from the dead warriors and stepping over their bodies with care. "Do you think the boarding party reached the bridge?"

Krin met my eyes. "The Raas will not be killed. He is a fierce fighter. No Zagrath can defeat him."

I loved Krin's blind confidence in his leader, but I knew that no one was invincible. Not even someone as huge and ferocious as Raas Kratos.

We went down another wide set of iron stairs, as we descended farther into the ship, dashing down a corridor and smack into a pair of Zagrath. Before Krin could stab at them, one of the soldiers grabbed him, pinning his arms to his side. Krin struggled and kicked and even slapped at him with his tail, but the enemy soldier was bigger, and obviously much stronger.

"Don't hurt him," I cried. "He's just a boy. He's not a warrior."

The other Zagrath twisted to face me, his laser rifle trained at my chest. "It's the woman."

"We found her," the other solider sounded triumphant as he held the still-wiggling Krin off the floor. "Call it in to command."

"Don't worry, citizen. We'll get you off this raider ship." The soldier in front of me lowered his rifle and pulled a small device off his belt. "Patrol three to command. We have the woman prisoner. Repeat. We have found the human prisoner and are bringing her back."

"Is that why you boarded the ship?" I asked. "To find me?"

The Zagrath holding Krin nodded. "If we didn't have to get you off, we could have just blasted it apart."

The other soldier eyed me and my torn dress. "You must know someone pretty high up to get this kind of rescue."

More like my sister had made some kind of deal with some Zagrath commander. I cringed to think what Tara had offered him in exchange for sending in the cavalry, and hated the ungrateful thoughts swirling through my head.

I didn't want to be rescued. I didn't want to go with these Zagrath soldiers. I didn't want to go back to my sister's ship.

The one closest to me let his rifle hang by his side as he took me by the elbow. "Are you injured? Did these brutes hurt you?"

I shook my head, my throat thick. Kratos had never hurt me—would never hurt me.

Remembering what he'd told me about not telegraphing my moves, I slumped against the soldier. "I feel faint."

He dropped his rifle to catch me, and the other soldier loosened his grip on Krin, who wiggled out of his grasp. I scooped the weapon from the floor, coming up and hitting the soldier trying to pick me up. The rifle cracked against his skull and he flew back, landing on the floor with a hard smack. The other soldier didn't figure out what was happening fast enough, his mouth dangling open as I rounded on him, hitting him on the side of the head with the butt of the gun. He dropped at my feet.

I glanced back at Krin, a grin splitting his face.

"I knew you were a fast learner," he said. "Not even the Raas would have thought of that."

I suspected playing the damsel in distress wasn't a technique Kratos had ever employed, or ever had to. I motioned down the corridor. "We'd better get out of here before these two wake up."

I could tell that Krin would have rather killed them, but he joined me in sprinting down the hall. When we reached another steep staircase, I paused.

"What's down there?"

"Escape pods."

"Perfect," I said. "No one will think to look for us in one of those."

When we got to the bottom of the staircase that was virtually a ladder, I surveyed the row of round, steel hatches. I peered through the clear window of one, and saw what looked like a small cockpit with room for two people. "We can fit in one of these."

Krin helped me open the hatch, stepping inside and taking one of the two seats facing the glass front that looked out over the pointed nose. Beyond the nose of the pod was another round door that appeared to spiral open. Beyond that, I knew, was space.

I stepped in after him and pulled the hatch closed behind me. The pod came to life, the controls illuminating, and a humming sound filling the small interior.

"Did you turn it on?" I asked, looking at Krin.

He shook his head vigorously. "I didn't touch anything. I swear."

"Maybe closing the hatch activated it," I said, joining him at the front. An illuminated pod with a running engine would not be as stealthy as I'd hoped. I scanned the controls, but didn't know the Vandar symbols. I'd never been great at anything having to do with spaceships, anyway.

The sounds of heavy thudding footsteps echoed from

behind us. Craning my neck around, I saw a pair of Zagrath soldiers looking in through the clear door.

"I think they found us," Krin said.

"Well, they're not going to get us." I turned back around, my gaze falling on a large, blue button. "Here goes nothing."

I slammed my hand on it. For a moment, nothing happened. Then the door in front of the pod spiraled open, and we rocketed out of the Vandar ship and into space.

"We did it!" I yelled, as we shot through a volley of laser fire.

Krin grinned at me, looking back at the Vandar ship and the Zagrath soldiers floating in space behind us. Then the pod jolted, and we started moving rapidly toward one of the Zagrath battleships.

THIRTY-TWO

Kratos

I swung my battle axe wide, catching a Zagrath soldier in the head, my blade embedding itself in the hard shell of his helmet. He shrieked as another axe plunged into his back, and he collapsed.

Bron put one boot on the soldier's back as he jerked his axe out of him, then he pulled mine out, as well.

I slapped my *majak* on the shoulder. "Good work. That's the last of them."

We were both heaving in breath as we stood on the wide platform outside the command deck. We'd beaten back the enemy soldiers who'd attempted to breech our controls and take the ship, and the bodies littering the steel floor at our feet were evidence of our victory. I could smell the char of burning metal and knew that our hull had taken damage, but at least our ship was still standing, and under Vandar control.

Corvak ran up from below, taking the stairs two at a time and causing them to rattle from the impact. "We have taken out all the Zagrath from the boarding party."

I nodded at him, noticing the blood smeared across his chest and dripping from his curved axe blade. Despite his disagreements with me, he would not fail me or his people. "We should see how the rest of the horde has fared."

We all strode back onto the command deck, the room loud with the sounds of incoming transmissions and alerts from damaged systems. I peered out the front of the ship and saw that the Zagrath battleship we'd been facing had backed away, smoke pouring from one side.

"Shields?" I barked, looking to my systems chief.

"Holding, Raas."

"Damage?"

"Nothing that cannot be repaired," another warrior told me, pride thick in his voice. "We caused more damage than we took."

"Good." I scraped a hand though my hair.

Bron walked to his console, scanning the readouts and glowering at the screen. "We did have an escape pod deploy during the battle."

"An escape pod?" I joined him at the console, squinting at the blinking alert. "One of the Zagrath?"

He shrugged. "Perhaps." He tapped his fingers across the smooth console, then twisted his head to look at me. "The guard outside your quarters missed his last check-in."

Despite the fact that I was sweating, a chill went through me. "Impossible."

Without waiting, I spun on my heel and ran off the command deck. The journey to my quarters had never seemed so long, as I thundered down staircases and tore down corridors, yelling for warriors to move out of my way.

When I reached the steel doors and the crumpled body lying in front of it, my heart plummeted.

I opened the doors and hurried inside, calling out for Astrid as I stormed the space, my gaze raking over every corner. She was not there.

Shaking my head in disbelief, I staggered back out, stepping over the warrior with the blaster wound in his chest and avoiding the dark puddle of blood shining on the dull, iron floor. The metallic scent was sharp in my nose, and I choked down the bile rising in my throat.

She would not have left me.

I continued through the ship, the smell of smoke getting stronger as I descended deeper into the shadowy belly of the vessel. My stomach was a knot of dread that hardened with each step.

Maybe she was hiding, like she'd done before when the ship was boarded. I scanned the hallways and any places large enough to conceal a small human, but she was nowhere. I spotted a wide swath of torn fabric that looked like one of her dresses, picking it up and holding it to my nose. It held the scent of my female, but I could not imagine why it would be ripped off and discarded in a corridor.

My throat tightened, as I imagined it being ripped forcibly off her. I held the scrap in one fist as I continued, passing the lifeless bodies of Zagrath soldiers sprawled on the floor. If the enemy had laid a hand on her, I would make them live to regret it.

Reaching the top of the stairs leading down to the escape hatches, I paused.

"Raas?"

I lifted my head to see Bron approaching from the other end of the long hallway. "You came to help me in my search."

He gave a single nod, although I saw in his eyes that he knew my search was fruitless.

We both descended the steep stairs, dropping down and shaking the floor. It took only a momentary glance at the row of pod hatches to see which one had been deployed. Bron strode over and tapped away at the control panel, while I peered through the clear door. Where there had been a pod, there was now nothing between the hatch and the external, circular door leading out into space.

"Well?" I asked, after his finger taps had slowed.

"The pod was deployed, but no destination was set."

A flicker of hope bloomed in my chest. "So, it could have been empty. Maybe the Zagrath deployed it to distract us?"

"It could have been the Zagrath, but it was not empty." He frowned, flicking his eyes to the hatch. "The pod was deployed from inside."

Whatever hope I'd had, shattered. She was gone.

I slammed my palm on the hatch, welcoming the sting of pain. "Is there any chance the Zagrath forced her into the pod?"

"We do not know it was her, Raas."

I slid my gaze to him, narrowing my eyes. "Do not humor me, *majak*. You have never done so before. I do not need it now."

He nodded, his cheeks coloring. "There is always a chance the Zagrath took her by force, Raas. We cannot be sure what happened. Only that her guard is dead, and she is missing."

"I lost her," I said in a near whisper.

Bron put a hand on my shoulder. "It is *not* done. Not yet."

I locked eyes with him, his determined expression making me straighten. The ache in my heart had already begun to morph into a blinding rage, the blood roaring in my ears. "No, it is not. If the enemy has what is mine, I will take it back. And destroy those who dared take from a Raas of the Vandar."

THIRTY-THREE

Astrid

"What's happening?" I pressed more buttons on the escape pod's control panel as we flew toward the Zagrath ship.

Krin's mouth was a hard line as he stared at the gray battleship looming ahead of us. "They're pulling us in."

"Like a tractor beam?" I knew some ships could use magnetic energy to hold ships in their orbit or pull them closer, but I'd never been on a ship high-tech enough to actually witness it.

He didn't answer, but I didn't need him to. From the stormy look on his small face, I knew there was no way to break free from whatever was drawing us closer to the Zagrath. No way to avoid being taken by them.

"They won't hurt us," I said, after a few moments of thought. "Especially if they think we fled the Vandar."

He swung his gaze to me. "You wish to tell the enemy that we ran from my people? That we are running *to* them?"

"They'll treat us differently if they think we escaped than if they think we never meant to leave the Vandar."

He folded his arms across his chest. "I would never betray my people." His gaze held mine in unspoken rebuke. "Or my Raas."

I huffed out a breath. "Do you think I want this? I was happy on the ship with your Raas. Okay, not until recently, but still, I didn't want to leave him. If I tell that to the Zagrath, though, they'll think I've been brainwashed or I'm crazy. The last thing I want is to end up in a padded cell on their ship. Then I'll never be able to get us out."

Krin's expression softened slightly. "You do not want to stay with the enemy who came to rescue you?"

I fought not to roll my eyes. "No way. I haven't taught you to make frosting yet."

A smile reluctantly teased the corners of his mouth, but he attempted to make his face stern. "You'll need my help to escape."

"Of course I will, so that means you're going to need to pretend to be trying to escape from the Vandar, as well."

He thought about this for a moment, his brows pressing together. Finally, he let out a sigh. "Fine, but only so I can help get us both back to my ship."

I held out my hand. "Deal."

He looked at my outstretched hand, and I remembered that Vandar did not shake. I dropped it and threw my arm around his shoulders instead. "I promise you we'll be off this Zagrath ship in no time."

His small body shuddered as our escape pod entered the side of the Zagrath battleship and landed with a thud on the floor of the hangar bay. I found myself humming a nameless tune, but even the usually comforting sound wasn't helping with the butterflies in my stomach. Especially when a squad of Zagrath soldiers in black helmets surrounded us, their laser rifles drawn.

"Ready?" I whispered to Krin, my hand hovering over the hatch release button.

He nodded, his face set in resignation. I knew the only reason he wasn't flying out of the pod with fists swinging was because of me.

I opened the hatch and held my hands in the air, nudging Krin to do the same. He grunted in displeasure as he lifted his arms up and walked out of the pod. I followed him, and we stood with multiple weapons trained on us.

Fast footsteps approached, the soldiers parting to let a Zagrath officer through. He was tall and slim, with light hair that looked like it was thinning on the top.

He appraised me and Krin, nodding as if pleased. "I am Commander Quijon of the Zagrath Empire. You are safe."

I forced myself to smile at him. "Thank you. I'm Astrid—"

"Yes, yes." He waved a hand at me. "We know who you are. Your sister made sure of that."

My heart beat a little faster. "Tara? Is she here?"

"No. She's been busy searching the sector for you, although I don't know how she thought she could find a Vandar horde in that ship of hers—or survive another encounter, if she did. It's hard enough for us, and we have the might of the empire at our disposal." His gaze went to my torn dress. "You look unharmed, if a bit disheveled. The Vandar didn't hurt you?"

"Not at all. I'm fine."

"Your sister will be glad to hear it, if we can reach her.

She's been out of communication range for nearly a full astro-day. No doubt hunting down some lead."

That sounded like Tara. "I'd love to talk to her when you're able to make contact."

The commander nodded. "That can be arranged. First, we'll need to debrief you both."

"You don't need to worry about him." I jerked a thumb at Krin. "He's just a kid who helped me escape. He doesn't know anything."

The commander eyed us, his gaze lingered over Krin. "He is still a Vandar. He might be able to give us valuable information about their ships, or their technology. We have never captured a Vandar before and been able to extract information from them."

The word 'extract' sent a tingle down my spine. "What do you mean? He's only a child. You can't interrogate a child."

Krin moved closer to me.

"He's a Vandar. It doesn't matter how old he is. If he's been living on their warship, he can be a valuable source of information, which could help us defeat the raiders, once and for all." The commander's eyes coolly shifted over Krin. "The Vandar are a scourge on the galaxy and a thorn in the empire's side. I am certain that in this case, the ends will justify the means."

I grabbed Krin's hand and squeezed it tightly. "I'm not going to let you torture him."

The Zagrath officer's lip curled. "You're defending one of them? They are a plague on the galaxy. Vermin we need to stomp out."

I cringed at the harshness of his words. No one deserved to be called vermin, especially not Krin. "Didn't you hear me? He helped me escape. He's the only reason I'm here and alive. I promise you he knows nothing about Vandar strategy."

"We'll see." The commander shrugged, flicking a hand toward us.

A pair of soldiers stepped forward, grabbing each of us by the arm. I slapped at the Zagrath's hand as he forced me away from Krin, his grip painfully tight on my arm. Krin saw my reaction and abandoned all promises to go calmly, kicking out at the soldier who'd grabbed him. When the Zagrath doubled over and loosened his grip, Krin spun and punched him hard in the gut.

I was still struggling to get away from the soldier who held me, when the commander stepped forward and pressed a metallic device to Krin's side, making the boy go rigid and then drop to the floor.

"What did you do to him?" I stared at the small, crumpled boy at my feet.

"Photon stunner." The commander's voice had not changed its level tone since he'd greeted us. "He'll be fine. I have no desire to kill him before we've gotten what we need from him."

"The Vandar are going to kill you when they find out what you've done to him." My voice shook, rage at the cruel commander coursing through me. "You'd better hope you can run far."

"Us, run?" The commander arched an eyebrow at me. "I do not think the Vandar will be coming after us to punish us for anything."

"What do you mean?"

"They're gone," he said.

I shook my head as the words sunk in. Gone? "Impossible. They wouldn't have left without..." I had been about to say that Raas Kratos wouldn't have left without me, but I stopped myself.

The commander smiled at me, but the warmth didn't

reach his eyes. "I'm afraid they did leave. Their horde of ships activated their invisibility shielding and vanished shortly before your pod reached us." He waved a hand toward space. "They ran like the rats they are. But don't worry. We'll find them and crush them, like we crush anyone who resists the empire."

For the first time, I really saw the Zagrath as the Raas had described them to me—cold, cruel, and interested in controlling everyone and everything. I blinked back tears, swallowing my urge to tell the Zagrath that the Vandar would never run. But I didn't know the truth. Maybe they did decide to cut their losses. Maybe the Raas had decided that it was better this way. We could never be together as true mates. He would have had to let me go, eventually. At least this way he would save his horde, and I knew that Raas Kratos valued his horde above all else—especially a female who could never be his true mate.

I squeezed my fists hard so that my nails bit into my flesh. I couldn't let the Zagrath see how heartbroken I was that the Vandar warlord had abandoned me. I lifted my chin and looked straight ahead as I was prodded along by the soldiers.

It didn't matter. As much as my heart ached, I needed to push my pain aside and focus on what mattered. I needed to figure out a way to save Krin and get him back to his people. I needed to bust us out of the Zagrath ship.

THIRTY-FOUR

Kratos

"You made the right decision, Raas." Bron faced me, as I paced a tight circle in my strategy room.

"Running?" I rounded on him. "When have the Vandar ever run?"

"I agree with the Raas," Corvak said from where he leaned against the wall, his bare chest still marred by streaks of enemy blood. "We should have stayed."

Bron shook his head. "It was an ambush. We were outgunned, and we could no longer fire on the lead battleship."

Corvak growled his disapproval. "We could have."

I shot him a look. "Not if it meant risking her life."

Corvak slapped a flat palm on the wall. "Why do you continue to protect her? She left you."

I flinched as if the slap had been on my flesh and not the

hard iron of the ship. I remembered what Astrid had warned me about my cousin, and I remembered her advice. "It does not matter. I cannot knowingly siege a ship she is on."

"We do not know she left of her own free will," Bron said. "It was in the midst of a battle, and there were many Zagrath soldiers hunting for her. It is likely they found her."

My blood boiled as I thought about my female being chased through the ship by enemy soldiers. My only comfort was the knowledge that the apprentice boy, Krin, was with her. He was missing from the ship and was not among the dead.

"None of that matters now," I said, squaring my soldiers. "Our horde took heavy damage. We must make repairs before we go after the Zagrath battleship."

Corvak looked up from wiping his wet blade on his battle kilt. "We are returning to battle?"

"The enemy took from us, from me," I said. "They have our apprentice, and they have my prize. I will not allow them to have either."

Corvak nodded his reluctant approval. The Vandar did not leave warriors behind, even young, apprentice warriors. I knew he would approve of that objective, even if he thought my desire to take back the female was misplaced. I also knew his hunger for more battle would outweigh his disapproval.

With Astrid's advice at the forefront of my mind, I leveled my gaze at my battle chief. "I trust you can get our horde battle-ready so we can chase down the Zagrath scum? No one can ready a horde like you can, cousin."

His cheeks colored slightly, then his mouth twitched into a menacing smile, no doubt as he imagined spilling more enemy blood. "You can count on me, Raas. I will assess our weapons and ready the horde for battle." He hooked his axe on his waist and backed quickly out of the room.

Crossing to the massive star chart, I studied our position and distance from the Zagrath. Bron had remained in the room.

"That was clever," he finally said. "He will fight even harder, now."

"It was the female's idea," I admitted. "She told me that I could diffuse his envy by making him feel more ownership of the horde."

"The female is advising you?" The curiosity was evident in his tone.

"Yes," I said, dreading his response.

"Maybe she should advise you more."

After a moment, I let out a breath. "Maybe you are right. I have led us into an ambush, and I refuse to blow up a Zagrath ship."

"We could not know it was an ambush, and I do not wish to see the female dead because she is on the enemy battleship. She deserves better than that."

I met his eyes. "I should have anticipated our enemy. That is my job as Raas."

"You are the Raas, not the god Lokken who forged the stars." He folded his arms across his chest. "Perhaps I should be most concerned about your ego, Kratos."

I smiled at that. "Do not worry. I always have you to keep me humble."

He inclined his head. "As always, your servant."

"If you do not think I made a tactical error, what makes you look at me like that?" I asked.

"It is clear she is more to you than a captive," my *majak* said. "I also know she cannot be what you need."

"How do you know what I need?" I glared at him, anger bubbling up inside me.

"You are the Raas." His voice was steady. "Tradition

dictates you take a mate in the old ways."

I turned back around, not willing to look on his face anymore. I knew what Vandar tradition decreed. I knew it better than anyone. But I also knew I could not control how I felt. I could not extinguish the heat she fired in my blood, or the desire that stormed through me every time I looked at her. I didn't care if she wasn't Vandar, or that she would never wear my mating marks. I didn't care about any of it.

"It is not law," I said, knowing my words were a feeble defense.

Bron was silent for a beat. "You would risk not having heirs? You would risk your position as Raas?"

His words were cold water dousing my fury, but they were right. I could not continue to rule as a Raas of the Vandar if I took a mate who did not share my marks. And I could only continue to pretend she was a prize I kept for pleasure for so long before my own horde would question me. They would not begrudge me a plaything, but it was becoming clear to all that she was more than that.

I leaned one hand against the clear chart. "I will take what you say under advisement, *majak*."

"Very well, Raas. I will check on our repairs and assemble the reports from the rest of the horde ships."

I made a noise in my throat in response, not watching as he left and the door swished behind him. When I was alone, I let my shoulders sag.

I shouldn't have been so surprised that Astrid was gone. I'd been foolish to think that the connection I'd felt between us would be enough to keep her with me, especially once she knew about the mating marks. I'd seen the look of betrayal in her eyes when I'd admitted the truth.

I pounded my hand on the clear star chart and it rattled. I never should have been honest with her about that. Whatever she might have felt for me had been wiped away with the knowledge that she could never be more to me than what she was now. She could never be my mate. She could never truly be my Raisa.

It had been cruel to call her that when I knew it was all a fantasy, although I hadn't imagined I was torturing anyone but myself. Even now, the word tasted bitter on my lips.

Raisa. A warlord's mate.

I could storm the Zagrath ship and get her back, but she could still never be my Raisa. She would just be Astrid, the small, pretty human who made me smile. I might be the Raas, with the power to take females as captives and do with them what I pleased, but I did not have the power to go against millennia of Vandar tradition.

I thought of my warriors, and the horde I'd led for so many years. They were my people and they deserved my strength and my loyalty. It was unthinkable that I would put a female—a human female—above them. I could not.

Squeezing my eyes shut, I gave a harsh shake of my head. I would lead my horde into battle against the Zagrath to retrieve our crew mate, but I would not bring the female back. Even though the thought made my heart feel as if it was being run through with a blade, I knew it was the right decision. She would go back to her sister's ship, and in time, I would forget her.

Dropping my gaze to my own chest, I glared at the marks I'd been born with, the marks that were determining my destiny and thwarting my happiness. Black and thin on the hard swell of my muscles, they were as much a part of me as the skin they swirled across. For one terrible moment, I wished I could claw them off with my bare hands and pretend they did not exist.

"Then they would think you are crazy," I muttered to

myself, knowing a Raas could never do such a thing. Not and remain Raas.

I thought of my father. I had not served under his brutal command and relentless tutelage to abandon my duty now. I had paid too high a price to be Raas, although I feared giving up Astrid would cost me even more.

"It is nothing I cannot survive," I told myself. "I am Vandar."

I pulled myself up to my full height and prepared to join my warriors on the command deck, giving a final malicious glance at my chest. My gaze caught on something, and I paused before leaving my strategy room.

Peering closer, my heart stuttered. A faint black swirl was appearing on my skin where it had not been before.

Mating marks.

THIRTY-FIVE

Astrid

"Not until you let me see my friend." I narrowed my eyes at the medic who was attempting to run some scans on me.

Even though he wore a Zagrath uniform, he didn't look like one of their automaton soldiers. He let out an exasperated breath. "You mean the Vandar who was rescued with you?"

"I mean the *child* who was with me." I couldn't bring myself to say that I'd been rescued. "He might be one of your enemies, but he's still just a kid, and I want to know where you took him."

I'd been brought to the ship's medical bay, but they hadn't brought Krin with me, despite my loud and vehement protests. Of the two of us, he'd been the one zapped, and he should have been checked out. Not me. I was fine. Pissed off, but fine.

I was only sitting on the shiny, metal, examination platform and breathing in the slightly antiseptic scent of the room because the door had been locked and there wasn't any point in me running around the examination stations that ran the length of the rectangular room. That, and I figured I had a decent chance of talking some sense into the medic.

"*I* didn't take him anywhere." The Zagrath medic waved his scanner over me, glancing down at the small screen. "All I know is that I'm supposed to check you out and make sure the Vandar didn't abuse you, or infect you with anything contagious."

I rolled my eyes and rubbed my hand across my chest where my skin felt warm. "Like I told the first guy, the Vandar didn't hurt me. They wouldn't."

He gave me a look like he thought I was delusional. "Yeah, because the raiders are known for being really great hosts."

I thought back to the soaking tubs in Kratos's quarters and the food he had brought to me every day, and then I remembered the Vandar guard who dutifully followed me and Krin around as I explored the ship. I knew better than to argue with this Zagrath, but a part of me really wanted to defend the Vandar. "So far, I've been roughed up more by your soldiers than I ever was by a Vandar."

The medic pressed his lips together as he studied his device, finally clearing his throat. He took a few steps over to a razor-thin screen that sat on a long white countertop, tapping his fingers on the screen. "You appear to be in perfect health."

"See?" I hopped down from the examination platform. "I told you the Vandar didn't hurt me."

He spun around. "I still need to take blood to be sure you weren't infected with any pathogens that don't show up on external scans."

I instinctively crossed my arms. I hated getting blood drawn. "The only way I'll let you take blood is if you agree to let me see Krin."

"I don't even know where he's being held."

The idea of the boy being held somewhere made me even more determined to see him. He would panic if he woke up in some sort of cell. I sized up the medic and decided to try another tactic.

"Listen." I took a step toward him and rested a hand on his arm. "You're the medical officer on the ship right? It's your job to make sure everyone on board is healthy."

He nodded at me, but looked skeptical. "That's right."

"Well, your commander stunned a little kid with a photon thingy. Shouldn't you at least check him out to make sure it didn't kill him?"

The Zagrath medic hesitated, biting his lower lip. "He used a photon stunner on a child?"

"Yep, and then dragged him off somewhere." I increased my pressure on his arm. "I only want to make sure he's okay. He did help me escape, after all."

"Really?" He blinked rapidly. "A Vandar kid helped you escape from their ship?"

"That's right. So, the least I can do is make sure he's okay. If you take me to see him and check him over, I'll let you take my blood without making a fuss."

After a moment, he exhaled loudly. "Fine, but do not make me regret this."

Just to seal the deal, I threw my arms around the guy and stood up on my tiptoes to give him a kiss on the cheek. "I promise I'll be a good girl."

I never would have been brave enough to attempt to this before I was taken by Kratos, but knowing how much he desired me made it easier to imagine that any male might.

The medic's cheeks flushed, and he cleared his throat again before pivoting back to the screen. His fingers flew across the smooth surface as he tapped rapidly. A schematic of the ship appeared with a small section illuminated in red.

He frowned. "They have him in a holding cell."

"Let's go." I tugged at his arm.

He didn't budge, but his gaze went up and down me. "You can't walk around the ship like that."

I glanced at my shapeless, torn dress. He had a point. I didn't exactly blend in. "Okay. I don't suppose you have a wardrobe department nearby."

He took long steps to a set of tall, inset, cabinet doors that were the same gleaming white as the rest of the room. He opened them and pulled out what looked like scrubs in the same steely-blue color as the Zagrath uniform. "Here. These are what I wear when I do surgery."

I took them, tugging the pants on under my dress and turning away from him as I whipped the dress over my head and pulled on the top. They were a bit baggy, but I tied the drawstring waist and tucked in the shirt. "Better?"

"Better." He went to the medical bay door and opened it by scanning his bare wrist, waving for me to follow him.

"Remind me why I'm doing this again," he muttered, as he led the way down the brightly lit corridors of the ship.

I rubbed at my chest again, wondering why my skin prickled with heat. "Because you're a medical professional concerned about the treatment of a child on board your ship."

He mumbled something I couldn't understand and walked faster, ducking into an empty elevator compartment.

Once the doors closed, we plunged down so fast I had to swallow a wave of nausea. The hallway we walked out onto was decidedly less bright and shiny than the upper levels, with lower ceilings, and even a dank smell.

"Do Zagrath ships have a dungeon level?" I asked, only partly kidding.

The medic didn't answer as he led me to the end where a guard stood outside an arched door.

"I'm here to check the prisoner," he said, his voice taking on an authoritative tone I hadn't heard before.

The guard sized him up then glanced back at me. "And her?"

"She's assisting me."

The guard apparently found my scrubs to be convincing, because he opened the door for us, stepping back as we entered.

The holding cell was every bit the jail cell, with a low, metal platform for a bed, and a pail in the corner. Krin was curled up on the hard steel slat, his eyes closed.

For a moment, my breath caught in my throat. Even though he was Vandar, he looked every bit the innocent little boy, with his knees and tail pulled into his chest and his small arms tucked under his head as a pillow.

I ran over to him. "Krin!" I knelt down and shook him gently. "Are you okay?"

The medic came up behind me, passing his scanner over the boy as Krin's eyes slowly opened.

"Astrid?" Krin looked dazed, no doubt a residual effect of the photon stunner.

"It's me." My voice cracked. "How do you feel? Are you in any pain?"

"I think that's my line," the medic said.

Krin's gaze shifted to the Zagrath, and his expression went from confused to hostile. "We're on their ship."

"It's okay," I whispered. "He's here to help you. He's a medic, and I convinced him to check you out. I was worried what that photon thing did to you."

Krin sat up, rubbing his head. "Photon? Is that why my head hurts?"

The medic glanced at his scanner. "It doesn't look like it did any permanent damage, but you did get a jolt, which is why your head hurts." He looked over his shoulder at the door. "I'm going to take you back to the medical bay. This isn't any place for a child who's recovering from a photon stunner."

The medic walked to the door, opening it and talking with the guard on the other side.

"Astrid," Krin whispered. "When can we get out of here?"

"I don't know," I told him. "Even if we get off the ship, we don't have anywhere to go. The Vandar horde left."

Krin stared at me, then shook his head. "They wouldn't leave us behind. Vandar don't leave warriors or mates behind —ever."

"Then they may come back for you," I said, only because I didn't want to take his hope away. "But I'm not a mate."

Krin tilted his head at me. "I've seen the way you and the Raas look at each other. I'm sure he will take you as his mate."

I shook my head, willing myself not to cry. "I know about the Vandar mating marks. I know your Raas can't take me as a mate because I will never have them."

Krin furrowed his brow, rubbing his temple with one hand and pointing to my chest with the other. "Then what is that?"

I looked down at the dark swirls on my skin curling up

from underneath the V-neck of the Zagrath scrubs. So that's why my skin felt so hot. I didn't know whether to laugh or to cry, so I did both.

The same marks that I'd seen so many times on Kratos's chest were now on mine. I had his mating marks.

CHAPTER
THIRTY-SIX

Kratos

I tightened the armor on my shoulder as I strode toward the hangar bay, the cool steel on my scorching flesh a steadying comfort. The ship buzzed with the anticipation of battle—warriors rushing by me with weapons ready and fury in their eyes. If they were surprised to see me so far from the command deck, they did not show it.

My own body vibrated as if I'd been electrocuted, and my heart pounded like a drumbeat matching my thundering steps as I clattered down a long staircase, leaping over the final two steps. If I thought too much about what I was doing, I would force myself to turn around. But there was no going back. Not now. Not anymore.

I wasn't sure if it was the physical change taking place within me, but my body burned as if I'd been struck by a fever. I touched a hand absently to the marks appearing on my chest, the skin hot. There was only one reason the dark swirls on my chest would grow. Astrid. As unbelievable as it was, I was getting mating marks because the human female was my one true mate. And I was going to go get her back.

The doors to the hangar bay were open when I approached them, warriors rushing in and out to prepare for our attack and ready our fighters. The expansive space that stretched nearly the width of the ship was filled with both revving ships and bustling warriors—so much so that my arrival went virtually unnoticed, just as I wished it to.

I breathed in the familiar scent of burning fuel as I walked purposefully toward a ship in the corner reserved for me—one of the few that didn't have its engine fired up. It was rarely used anymore, but I liked to keep it in case I wanted to test my flying chops. Putting a palm on the black hull, I appraised the sleek vessel. Like all of the Vandar ships, it resembled a bird in many ways—curved, outstretched wings and a nose like a beak—but with menacing stealth panels instead of feathers.

"I take it you're inspecting the ships before battle?"

Bron's voice behind me was not a total surprise. If anyone would guess my mind, it would be him. Still, the blood roaring in my ears told me I did not have time for my *majak's* counsel.

"You know I am not," I said, without turning.

"Do you think it wise to leave the ship before battle, Raas?"

I clenched my hand resting on the ship into a fist, trying to control my impatient rage. "I have no choice."

"There is always a choice."

I spun to face my *majak*. "What do you call these?" I gestured to my chest and watched his eyes widen.

"Mating marks," he whispered. "Because of the human?"

I scowled at him. "Who else?"

He shook his head. "How could this happen? She is not Vandar."

"I do not know, but it has happened. It cannot be ignored." I did not tell him that the way my flesh burned, there was no way I could ignore them even if I wished to. "It is done."

Bron nodded mutely. He looked as startled and confused as I had been when the reality of the marks appearing on my skin had finally hit me. And everything he said was right. It should have been impossible. It had never happened before.

I closed the gap between us and clapped a hand on his arm. "I must go after her and bring her back. She is no longer just my prize and my possession. She is mine in every way, and I will not allow the Zagrath to take what is meant to be mine forever."

Bron seemed to recover his senses. "What is your plan?"

I glanced back at the ship. "Fly in undetected. Get inside, find her and the boy, and use the distraction of our attack to bring them home."

He went to a standing console, his finger tapping on the screen. "I will tell Corvak so he knows to create a diversion for us."

"Us?" I shook my head. "I am doing this alone."

Bron's lips became thin white lines as he pressed them together. "I would be a very bad *majak* if I allowed my Raas to fly into the belly of the beast alone."

"As my *majak*, you should be here, leading the battle."

"Corvak can lead the battle better than I could. It is as natural to him as breathing."

I knew he was right about that. No one could direct war like my battle chief.

Bron took long steps past me to the ship, activating the

entry hatch. "I told him he has the command deck. It is done."

When the steel ramp hit the floor, I stomped up it, pausing and twisting around. I leveled my gaze at my most trusted warrior. "When this is over, we should talk about your insubordination."

His mouth twitched slightly, and he inclined his head. "Yes, Raas."

The interior of the ship was as black as the outside, with only two seats and a small space for extra warriors to stand. It was not the type of ship we used for boarding parties, but its speed and small size made it perfect for a covert mission.

Sinking into one of the seats, I engaged the engine with a flip of a switch. Bron took his place next to me, and we began working together without a word, checking systems and preparing to take off. For a moment, it felt like we were new warriors again, flying together as we had in more battles than I could remember. My fingers tingled as they moved easily over the controls, working from muscle memory, and I realized how much I'd missed being in the middle of the action.

Being Raas meant I spent my time on the command deck and in my strategy room, planning out attacks. Even if I sometimes joined raiding missions, it was rare that I would fly in a battle. My pulse quickened, and I let out a rumble that matched that of the throaty engine.

"Systems ready," Bron said, his voice vibrating with excitement.

With a quick glance around me, I gunned the engines, and we rocketed across the now-clear deck and out the wide mouth into space. Spotting the Zagrath battleship some distance away, I engaged our invisibility shielding and increased speed. The enemy had no idea my horde was so close, watching them and waiting to attack.

As we approached the massive gray battleship, an explosion rocked the hull, the blast even sending my vessel briefly backward.

I peered down at my console and cursed. "Corvak has started the attack."

"*Tvek!*" Bron slammed his hand onto his armrest. "He knew to wait."

"Corvak has never been good at waiting."

Bron grunted. "I hope he does not blow up the ship before we can get our people off it."

I hoped the same thing, as I rocketed toward the enemy ship, dodging weapons fire. I maneuvered our ship unseen into the Zagrath hangar bay, setting it down out of the way of the ships preparing to take off.

I stood and put a hand to the hilt of my axe. "That was the easy part."

THIRTY-SEVEN

Astrid

"What was that?" I grabbed for the edge of the examination platform, as the ship lurched to one side.

Krin gripped the platform where he was sitting, glancing up as red lights began to flash overhead. The medic who'd gotten Krin released to his care stumbled to the side, holding his arms out for balance, the scanner in his hand almost slipping out of his grasp.

"It feels like we took a hit," he said, when he'd righted himself and resumed scanning Krin.

"As in, we were attacked?" My heart fluttered with excitement, which would normally have been a strange reaction to finding out the ship you were in was under attack. But if we were under attack, I knew who it was. Kratos was coming for us.

Krin met my gaze and smiled at me. He didn't need to say a word to tell me that he'd been right. The Vandar would not leave a warrior behind. Or a mate.

I touched the marks that were curling up my collarbone, knowing they were there without looking at them because my skin felt like it was on fire. I couldn't explain how it had happened, or how it was possible, but there was no question that I was developing the exact marks that Kratos had on his skin. Only Kratos had never mentioned that getting them would make my skin burn.

Krin hadn't seemed surprised when he'd pointed them out. Actually, he'd acted like he'd expected it all along, even though I don't know how he could have. Not even Kratos had believed it possible.

"Are we safe here?" I scanned the medical bay and tried to put my hot skin out of my mind. Aside from the one standing tray of tools the medic had beside him, everything was tucked away in cabinets and drawers. I assumed this was because we were on a battleship and flying medical implements would not be a good thing.

"Perfectly," the medic said. "This battleship has withstood many battles."

"Even from a Vandar horde?" Krin asked.

The Zagrath flinched. "Why do you think the hit came from a Vandar? We just beat them back."

Krin shrugged. "The Vandar never leave a warrior behind."

The medic darted a glance at him and then at me. "Maybe I should alert the commander that there may be an attempt to take you both off the ship."

I stepped in front of him as he made a move toward the

standing console. "I wouldn't disturb the commander right now. Don't you think he has his hands full? Besides, how could the Vandar get us off the ship?"

His shoulders relaxed. "You're right. Their warriors could never board our ship without our knowledge." His gaze went to the door. "Still, it would be better if I requested a guard or two. Just to be on the safe side."

I put both hands on his chest to keep him from moving. "Guards? Does this mean you don't trust me?" I attempted my best sad face. "I thought we were friends."

His brows lifted, the confusion clear on his face.

"Have I attempted to escape?" I motioned my head toward Krin. "Has he?"

"Well, no."

"We walked all the way with you from the holding cell to the medical bay without any guards," I said. "Do you really think we'd try something now?"

"I don't know," he stammered. "I guess not."

I fluttered my eyelashes at him, even though I felt ridiculous doing it. "I promise you I have no desire to be anywhere else on this ship but right here with you."

His cheeks flushed, and he cleared his throat. "I guess there's no point in pulling a guard away from his duty."

I walked my fingers up his chest. "Not if they're going to disturb us."

"Disturb us?" The red of his cheeks deepened, and he peered over his shoulder at Krin.

I took advantage of his momentary distraction to snatch one of the scanners from the standing tray and knock him over the head with it. He stumbled for a moment, and I realized I hadn't hit him hard enough. Luckily, Krin grabbed another scanner and hit him again, this time harder. The medic dropped to the floor.

I let the scanner clatter to the floor after him. "We didn't kill him, did we?"

Krin hopped down from the examination platform, bending over him. "He's alive. His head might hurt when we wakes up, but I don't think he'll have worse than that." He tilted his head back to look at me. "I was right that you'll make a good Vandar."

I huffed out a breath, not sure if that was the kind of compliment I wanted. I'd just knocked out the only Zagrath who'd been nice to me. I swiveled around, opening drawers. "We should tie him up. I don't know how long he'll be out, and it would be great if he didn't tip off the other Zagrath before we get off this ship."

I located a few rubber ties used to make tourniquets and managed to bind the medic's hands at the small of his back, while Krin searched for anything we could use as a weapon.

He slammed a drawer shut and threw his hands into the air. "No blasters."

"Well, it is a medical bay. They probably discourage things that can kill you."

"I do not understand the Zagrath."

I almost laughed at the boy's fierce expression. "Don't worry. We might not need a weapon. We just need to look like we know where we're going." I picked up the scanner from the floor and gestured to the scrubs I wore. "I already look like I'm one of their medical staff. If we get stopped, I can say I'm taking the prisoner for tests."

He glowered at me. "I'm the prisoner?"

"You have a better plan?"

"Yes." He crossed his small arms over his chest. "I find a battle axe and slash my way through the ship until we find our escape pod."

"Why don't we call that plan B, until we happen to find a battle axe?"

He let out a tortured sigh. "We will do it your way for now."

"Thank you." I led him to the door, but it didn't open. I touched the panel to the side, but nothing.

Of course. The door was locked from the inside and only authorized Zagrath could enter or exit. I thought back to the medic waving his wrist over the panel to open the door, then I peered over my shoulder at his inert body on the floor. Just great.

"We have to wave his wrist over the panel to get out," I told Krin, rubbing at my burning chest.

Krin nodded and went to one of the drawers he'd previously opened, pulling out a thin scalpel. "I'll cut it off if you hold him down."

I snatched the blade from him and dropped it back in the drawer. "We're not cutting off his wrist! We're going to lift it high enough to activate the panel."

Krin huffed out another breath. "Cutting it off would be easier."

Shaking my head, I scooped my arms under the medic's shoulders and dragged him across to the door. I stood and caught my breath. He looked slim, but he was still heavy. I quickly untied his hands, hoping he wouldn't come to.

When his arms flopped free, I pointed to Krin. "When I lift him up, I need you to hold his wrist to the panel. Got it?"

"Got it," Krin said, although I knew he'd rather be holding a severed wrist to the panel.

I heaved the body up as high as I could, and Krin pulled his arm and wrist even higher. The panel blinked, and the door swished open. I stuck my foot in the opening as I hurriedly retied the medic's hands.

"Let's go," Krin said, stepping out into the corridor.

I joined him outside the medical bay as the doors closed. I hadn't had time to push the medic out of sight, but if we were lucky, no one would visit the medical bay anytime soon.

I turned and almost walked into a pair of Zagrath soldiers, one supporting the other as they both staggered forward, their uniforms charred. They paused outside the medical bay, waving their wrists to open it and then gaping at the bound medic on the floor.

Their heads swiveled to Krin and me as we backed away. Then Krin grabbed my hand, and we both started to run.

Apparently, we weren't so lucky.

THIRTY-EIGHT

Kratos

" I have never been on a Zagrath battleship, Raas," Bron said, as we ducked behind a row of steel barrels on the hangar bay.

After disembarking from our vessel, we'd been darting between ships and behind anything that would hide us from the pilots and crew running around in the wide space.

"Nor have I," I told him. "I do not think we dressed for the occasion."

He choked back a laugh, glancing down at our distinctive Vandar battle kilts and bare chests, then at our long tails behind us. One look at the humanoid imperial soldiers in their stiff uniforms told us that we would not go unnoticed.

Spotting a pile of grimy fabric drop cloths, I snatched one from the top and handed another to Bron. "Put this around your shoulders."

I unfurled mine and wrapped it around myself, glad that it extended far enough that my bare legs were not noticeable. The scratchy fabric made the hot skin around my mating marks even more irritated, and I gritted my teeth.

Bron wrinkled his nose as we both held the dirty, gray fabric closed at our throats. "This smells like it was soaked in engine fuel."

I sniffed, inhaling the sharp, chemical smell. "Then let us avoid flames."

We moved along the edge of the space until we reached the wide doors, passing through them and into the corridor without being seen. I immediately flinched as my eyes adjusted to glaring light overhead, red bursts of light flaring every few seconds.

I'd taken plenty of Zagrath freighters and shuttles and transports, but I'd never actually walked around one of my enemy's battleships. Aside from being too bright, there were no exposed beams or framing like on Vandar ships. Instead, the walls were smooth, pale gray, and arched so that it felt like walking through a tube.

I instantly missed the open catacombs of my ship and the wide stairs that led you from level to level. On this ship, you could not see anything but the hall you were on and had no idea where it led.

"How will we locate them?" Bron asked me, looking down both sides of the long hall.

"We need to find an access point to their systems." I motioned for him to follow me as I picked a direction and began to walk.

Bron craned his head toward the hangar bay doors. "And remember how to get back here. I suspect all their corridors look the same."

The thumping of running feet made us exchange a

nervous glance. I put a hand on the hilt of my battle axe, but Bron pulled me down a smaller corridor as the soldiers rushed by.

"It would be best if we did not attract attention just yet," he said, his gaze focusing on a panel in the wall. "Let me see what this might tell us."

We both shed the drop cloths then I stood guard, my axe at the ready, as Bron pulled a device from his belt and scanned the panel with it. "Anything?"

His head was bowed as he read the small screen. "I'm getting the ship's schematics. Once that's downloaded, I'll look for where they logged in their most recent visitors."

I made a low noise in my throat. I knew Astrid was somewhere on the enemy ship. My body tingled at the nearness of her, my pulse racing.

"The holding cells," Bron said, then held up a finger. "But not anymore."

I swung my head to him. "The holding cells? They are treating her like a prisoner?"

"Not the female. Just the boy." He swiped his finger across the screen. "Her they took to the medical bay."

My heart lurched. "Was she injured?"

Bron looked up at me, his brows pressed together. "It does not say."

A sound behind us made me turn on the spot. Two Zagrath fighters in full uniforms and helmets had rounded the corner. One held his wrist up to a door panel and the door swished open while the other had spotted us and seemed frozen in shock. I guessed two bare-chested Vandar raiders in battle kilts were not what he'd been expecting.

Before Bron could react, I swung my axe up, hitting one of the Zagrath with the flat side of the blade and knocking him out. When the other swung his laser rifle up to fire, I used it to jerk him toward me, spinning him around and giving his neck a sharp snap. He also collapsed onto the floor.

"We should probably hurry," I told Bron.

I'd purposefully killed the soldiers without spilling blood, so I dragged one over to a doorway and jammed him into it, doing the same with the other Zagrath and another recessed doorway.

"I've got what we need." Bron held up his device, eyeing both slumped-over corpses.

"We need to get to the medical bay." I swallowed down my panic that my mate might be hurt. At least I knew the Zagrath would treat her well, since she was human, like them. Then I thought about our young Vandar apprentice in a Zagrath holding cell, and my anger flared anew. Of course, the empire would treat a child like a criminal. "Then we go to the holding cells."

If my *majak* disagreed with my strategy, he didn't say it. Instead, he jerked his head toward the fallen soldiers. "We need a way to get through doors."

Without hesitation, I brought my blade down again, slicing off one of the Zagrath soldier's hands below the wrist.

"That should do it." He nodded toward a nearby corridor. "We go this way."

We left the drop clothes on the floor. They were little disguise, since nothing about us looked remotely Zagrath. Walking quickly, we passed through a series of corridors that seemed to be deserted. It didn't take me long to understand that Bron was taking us through back passageways, away from the main part of the ship. When we reached a set of doors at the end of a hallway, I held the bloody wrist to a flat panel to one side, and they parted to reveal a small compartment.

I knew elevators from other ships, but I did not like them. They made warriors slow and lazy. I reluctantly got on and it surged up, making my stomach plummet. Another reason I despised the contraptions.

"We will arrive near the medical bay," Bron told me as the elevator slowed, reaching for his own battle axe. "We should be ready."

The doors opened and we rushed out with our weapons drawn. I did not see any Zagrath, but I could hear them. Flattening myself to the wall, I edged forward. The voices from around the corner were raised and angry.

"What happened here?"

"I am not certain, Commander." The second voice shook. "I was assessing the Vandar child when—"

"The Vandar child was here? I ordered him sent to a cell!"

"Yes, but the woman convinced me that he needed to be checked over." The second Zagrath's voice sharpened. "He was injured by a photon stunner."

Bron tensed next to me. They'd used a photon weapon on the boy? I bit back a growl and forced myself not to leap out and attack the commander.

"So? It doesn't matter that he's a child," the commander nearly shrieked. "He's a Vandar raider."

"I'm a medical professional. It's my job to treat everyone, regardless of species. Especially a child."

"Well, where are your patients now?"

There was a heavy pause, and I held my breath.

"They must have knocked me out. When I came to, a Zagrath soldier was untying my wrists."

The commander sighed. "I am starting to regret punishing the Lussites mercenaries for their attempt to kill the target instead of bringing her to me. I don't have time to deal with any of this now. We're taking heavy fire from the raiders. It's not as if the woman can fly an escape pod off the ship. We'll track her down once we defeat the Vandar."

Bron tugged my arm, and we backed away from the medical bay. Even though I was on an enemy ship and had no idea where Astrid or our apprentice were, a feeling of warmth fluttered in my chest and replaced the burning anger. She'd tricked the medic to get the boy out of the cell, and then attacked him to escape. She hadn't run to the Zagrath willingly. She'd been taken here, and she was trying her best to get off the ship and back to me.

After we were in the elevator again and could speak freely, Bron turned to me. "Where do you think she'd go, Raas? You know her better than anyone."

"She may not be able to pilot an escape pod off the ship, but I would not put it past her to attempt to steal one of the Zagrath ships."

Bron angled his head at me. "Can she fly one?"

"No." I touched a finger to my marks. "But trust me, she is more determined than she looks."

The elevator doors slid open, and a group of Zagrath fighters stared at us, their laser rifles aimed at our chests.

CHAPTER
THIRTY-NINE

Astrid

"How would I know?" I looked down at the controls of a Zagrath shuttle. "I told you, I'm not a pilot. I only ever did navigation, and I was pretty bad at it."

My hands shook, and my mouth felt like I'd swallowed cotton—sensations I hadn't experienced since I'd left my sister's ship. Working on the bridge had often made me so nervous I'd get clammy palms or the jitters, but I'd hoped I'd left that behind when I'd left the freighter. I guessed not. I hummed to myself in an attempt to calm my nerves, but even my humming was shaky, and my burning skin wasn't helping things.

"Fuck, fuck, fuck," I whispered. That seemed to help, so I continued to say fuck over and over.

Krin sat next to me in the small cockpit, one leg bouncing up and down. My cursing obviously wasn't doing anything for his nerves. "You must know *something*. If we don't get this ship moving soon, the Zagrath are going to find us."

I blew out a long breath. "Don't worry," I said, more to myself than to him. "We picked the oldest, most beat-up shuttle they have. I'm sure this is the last thing they'd want to use in a battle."

The boy cast his gaze around the worn cockpit. "Are we sure it can fly?"

I wasn't, but I hoped the Zagrath wouldn't have a completely useless vessel sitting on their hangar deck. It hadn't been in the repair area. "Of course, it can fly," I told him with more confidence than I felt. I put a hand on his bouncing leg to still it. "We've made it this far, haven't we?"

He met my eyes, finally nodding. We'd managed to wind our way through the ship without being stopped or questioned. It helped that the Zagrath were in the midst of a battle, and that I'd made Krin pretend to be wounded so that I looked like a medic taking him for treatment. At least, that was what we'd hoped it looked like, and the soldiers rushing by us had been too distracted to notice or care.

"Don't worry, Krin. I promise I'll get us home."

Home. Did I really think of the Vandar ship as home? It seemed bizarre that I could be more comfortable on a raider warbird with its dark shadows, labyrinth of iron stairs and open passageways, and constant echo of warriors bellowing to each other. But I knew the Vandar were more than these things, and Raas Kratos was definitely not the brutal warlord the galaxy thought he was. At least, not to me.

My pulse quickened as I thought about the imposing Raas, his dark eyes flashing as he looked at me. I knew he was out there on the Vandar warbird, and I knew the horde had returned for me and Krin. As much as the Vandar despised the Zagrath Empire, I believed Krin. The Vandar never left a warrior behind. Or a mate.

My heart fluttered in my chest. I should probably be freaked out that black tattoos were appearing on my skin and marking me as the mate of Raas Kratos, but I wasn't. Aside from the burning sensation I hoped was temporary, the thought of being his—*really* being his—thrilled me. My heart was already his and I think it had been for a while, so I was glad my body had caught up.

I narrowed my eyes at the controls again. I just needed to figure this out, and I could get back to him.

"Come on, Astrid," I whispered to myself, hearing my sister's voice in my own head. "This is not that hard. You know this."

Tara had said the same thing to me in some variation probably a thousand times. Usually, it made me cringe because I knew it shouldn't be that hard. I also knew that ships—flying them, navigating them, fixing them—had never been my jam. Not like they'd been Tara's. Another way we were completely different.

"You okay?" Krin asked me.

"What?" I saw the concerned look on his face and realized that me talking to myself was probably not all that comforting. I closed my eyes and steadied my breath. I had to do this, for Krin, if no one else. The Zagrath would definitely toss him back in a cell if they caught us.

"Maybe the Raas can fly it," Krin said, interrupting my thoughts.

"I'm sure he could," I muttered, opening my eyes, "but he's not exactly here right now."

"Sure, he is." Krin pointed a small finger out the side of the cockpit's wraparound window.

Leaning forward, I peered across him toward the wide, hangar bay doors. My mouth gaped open. That was definitely Raas Kratos swinging his battle axe over his head, while his first officer fought off Zagrath soldiers by his side.

"How did they get here?"

Krin just grinned broadly. "I told you they wouldn't leave us behind."

Even though there were considerably more Zagrath soldiers, the Raas and his *majak* were quickly dispatching them, even fending off blaster fire with their circular axe blades. Watching them slash and duck, almost moving in unison, made it hard for me to close my mouth again. I stared openly for a few moments before Krin nudged me.

"*Vaes.*"

"What do you mean, *vaes*? Where are we going?" I waved a hand at the cockpit. "We're the only ones in a ship."

Krin shook his head at me, as if he was disappointed in me. "Just because you can't see the Vandar ship, doesn't mean it isn't here."

"The invisibility shielding?" I looked out across the hangar bay again, searching for signs of an invisible spaceship. My gaze caught on something at the far end, a rippling of the light. "There." I pointed to the area. "Is that it?"

Krin followed my finger, his eyes brightening. "I think so. That's probably where the Raas and his *majak* are heading. If we want to get off with them, we'd better go now."

I followed the boy, rushing out of the Zagrath ship and making a beeline for the Vandar ship we couldn't see. Out of the corner of my eye, I spotted Kratos and Bron fighting their way across the hangar bay. More Zagrath had joined the fray, but they were easily felled.

I desperately wanted to call out to Kratos and let him know that I was okay, but I knew better than to disturb him in the middle of a battle. Instead, I kept running around ships and dodging startled Zagrath crew as they repaired vessels or prepared to board fighters. When we were almost halfway across the expansive space, sirens began to blare overhead.

"They know we escaped," I yelled to Krin.

He craned his neck back to look at me, jerking a thumb toward the Raas. "They know they have Vandar intruders."

He was right. More Zagrath soldiers streamed through the hangar bay entrance and headed right for Kratos and Bron. My stomach clenched at the sheer number of well-armed fighters.

I grabbed Krin's arm and brought him to a sudden stop. "We have to help them."

He saw the Zagrath reinforcements and his small jaw tightened. "I don't have any weapons."

My gaze scoured the hangar bay for anything we could use, but there was nothing that could match a blaster. We might be able to throw a bunch of wrenches at them, but chances were good we'd end up being shot or taken captive before we could do any real damage.

"I have an idea." I tugged him with me as I ran even faster toward the invisible Vandar ship. "Can you get us on the ship even though we can't see it?"

He nodded, but his expression was wary.

"Don't worry," I yelled over the wail of the sirens. "I'm not going to try to fly it. We just need to create a distraction."

Krin grinned. "I'm good at distractions."

When we reached the area where the light shimmered strangely, Krin pressed his hands to the invisible ship until he reached some sort of latch. As the ramp lowered, I could see the inside of the Vandar ship, which was not covered in special shielding.

Krin and I hurried up the ramp and ran to the cockpit. Peering out the front, I saw that the nose of the ship was pointed toward the battle raging between the two Vandar warriors and the dozen Zagrath.

"Perfect," I muttered under my breath.

Krin engaged the engines, clearly more familiar with Vandar vessels than with enemy ones. "What's your idea for a distraction?"

The sound of the siren was muffled inside the ship, but I still had to raise my voice. "I'm going to shoot at them."

Krin's gaze went out the front of the ship to where the fight was getting closer to us, then he blinked at me a few times. "I thought you weren't good with ships."

I glanced back at the fight in time to see Raas clutch his side, although he did not lower his axe. He'd been hit. Sweat poured off both warriors, and blood ran down Bron's face. The Zagrath were advancing and more soldiers were rushing in behind them. As skilled as Kratos and Bron were, I knew even they couldn't fight them all off.

I gritted my teeth. "I have to do something to save them. They can't die on a Zagrath ship." And I couldn't bear watching Kratos die in front of me. Not after he'd believed in me and listened to my counsel and made me feel valuable for the first time in a long time. I didn't care if he was a Raas of the Vandar, feared throughout the galaxy and notorious for leaving a wake of death and destruction. He was *my* Raas.

Krin's face darkened at the thought. "Do it."

I studied the console for a moment, hoping that the weapons were located in the same place on all alien ships. I tapped a few buttons and laser cannons emerged on either side of the cockpit. I aimed a little beyond the Zagrath soldiers—in case my aim was bad—closed my eyes, and fired.

"Woo hoo!"

I opened my eyes to Krin's screams, peeking out the front of the ship and seeing a massive smoldering hole in the hangar bay. I hadn't missed, but it looked like I'd blown up a quarter of the hangar bay. Zagrath soldiers lay scattered around the blackened blast zone, some staggering to their feet. I couldn't see the Raas or Bron through the haze, and my heart sank.

Billowing smoke filled the air, and I could taste the bitter char as I swallowed. I was too terrified to ask Krin if the Raas had been hit, my heart hammering in my chest louder than the sirens. I rubbed at my eyes as the smoke stung them, tears pricking the backs of my eyelids.

He wasn't dead. He couldn't be.

I turned to ask Krin, but the words died in my throat when I saw the stunned expression on his face, his eyes focused slightly behind me.

Suddenly, I was being lifted out of my seat, large arms wrapping around me as Raas Kratos crushed me to him.

"Raisa," he murmured. "It's really you."

"It's me," I said between choked sobs, twisting around so I could look up at him, hardly believing he was really holding me. "I've been trying to get back to you."

He pulled away from me, locking eyes with me and cupping my face in both of his large hands. "I know. I've been trying to find you."

Bron pushed past both of us, sinking down into the pilot's chair. "If you two don't mind, I'm going to get us out of here before the Zagrath figure out what happened." He shook his own head as if trying to dislodge something. "*Tvek*, I don't even know what just happened."

"Astrid blew up the Zagrath," Krin said, his voice brimming with pride.

As the ship rumbled across the enemy hangar bay and burst out into space, Kratos smiled at me. "I knew you were my most valuable crew mate."

CHAPTER
FORTY

Kratos

The battle was still raging when we returned to the ship, and I was grateful when Bron successfully piloted us through the glowing volley of laser fire. As much as I hated it, I knew I had to leave Astrid and report to the command deck.

When we walked down the ship's ramp, she glanced at the scorch mark in my side, evidence of a Zagrath blaster grazing my flesh. "I don't suppose I can convince you to get that looked at?"

Bron came down after us, the gash in his forehead now only trickling blood instead of oozing it.

Astrid grimaced. "Or that?"

I pulled her to me again, loving the feel of her body against mine. It was like I needed to have as much of her skin on mine as I could to prove she was real, and she was with me.

"I didn't think so." She sighed, pulling away and gazing at me. "In that case, you should go kick some more Zagrath ass."

My eyes went from hers down to the black lines curling across her skin. I traced one of the swirls with my finger, savoring the look of my mating marks on her. Without meaning to, I emitted a low growl.

Astrid placed her hand on top of mine, entwining our fingers. "I'll be waiting for you when the battle is won. I'm not going anywhere, Raas."

I tightened my hand around hers. "You are mine. You have always been mine."

She gave me a shy smile. "And now it's official."

"It is done." I had never meant the Vandar oath as much as I did at that moment. The thought that the small female who'd flamed my desires was my true mate sent a rush of need pounding through me and made my cock swell. I crushed my mouth to hers, parting her lips and devouring the taste of her. Her small breathy moan made my head swim as our tongues tangled, and I dragged a hand through her hair, tipping her head back and kissing her deeper.

Only the loud thumping of boots forced me to tear myself from her. I pulled back, panting.

Corvak did not comment on the female or our wounds as he joined us. "More Zagrath ships have appeared Raas. It seems they sent for reinforcements."

His words instantly doused my euphoria. I straightened and gave him a curt nod. "I will join you on the command deck."

When I looked down at Astrid, she was already waving

me away. "Go. I'll be fine." She motioned her head toward the apprentice boy. "I've got Krin."

I was grateful she understood me so well, and was not threatened by the demands of me being Raas. I lifted her palm to my lips and kissed it, letting my lips linger and my eyes hold hers for a long moment. "I will return to you soon."

With that, I spun and rushed out with Bron and Corvak flanking me. I glanced at my battle chief as we hurried through the ship, taking stairs three at a time and leaping from one suspended walkway to the other. "What are our damages so far?"

"Our shields have held, but other ships in the horde have not been so lucky." His hands were in tight fists by his side. "The lead Zagrath ship has been relentless. The only reason I did not retaliate harder was because you and Bron were on it."

I noticed that he didn't mention Astrid, but I didn't let that bother me. He did not yet know that we had developed the mating marks and that she was truly my mate and would be my Raisa—and his.

We burst onto the command deck, the warriors barely hearing our arrival over the cacophony of static-filled reports coming in from the rest of the horde ships and the shrieking alarms of incoming weapon fire. Out the front of the ship, I saw the Zagrath battleship I'd been on not long ago—gray and hulking. I thought of the commander who'd sent an injured child to a holding cell.

"Fire on the lead ship," I ordered. "Everything we've got."

There was no hesitation. A stream of red laser fire erupted from underneath the belly of our warbird, hitting the enemy ship and making it shudder. A torpedo impacted one side and exploded, sending parts of hull spiraling into space.

The Zagrath ship immediately returned fire and our ship shook from the impact.

"Shields holding, Raas," Bron called, from where he stood at his console.

"Should I prepare a raiding party?" Corvak asked, his voice nearly vibrating. "Once we have disabled the lead ship, we should be able to strip it quickly." His upper lip curled into a sneer. "And kill more Zagrath."

Before I could answer him, a massive explosion rocked the ship, sending us both sprawling on the floor. I pulled myself up, scanning the command deck and seeing that no one was wounded and there was no visible damage.

"Report," I bellowed. "Casualties?"

One of my warriors clutched the sides of his console with white knuckles. "None, Raas. Our ship wasn't hit."

When I looked out the front of the ship, I saw what had been hit and why we'd felt it. The lead Zagrath ship was no more. It had been destroyed. Chunks of the hull were flying past us, and the sky was littered with debris from the blast.

"*Tvek!*" I swiveled my head to Bron. "Did we—?"

"No, Raas. At least, it wasn't all us. From what I can tell, the Zagrath were also being fired upon by a ship from behind."

Corvak got to his feet, his face a mask of confusion. "None of our horde has moved behind the enemy ships."

"Raas?" One of my warriors turned to me. "You're being hailed."

"Hailed?" I glanced again at the remnants of the Zagrath ship.

He nodded, his eyes wide. "By Raas Kaalek of the Vandar."

Corvak sucked in a breath next to me. He knew my brother as well as I did.

I squared my shoulders and clenched my fists. "On screen."

The view of space vanished, replaced by a Vandar warrior who looked strikingly similar to me. With jet-black hair that fell long and straight down his back and identical dark eyes, Kaalek looked much as I remembered him. The leather guards capping his shoulders like scales and the thick, black leather straps crisscrossing his chest from both sides were new. Then again, I had not laid eyes on my brother since he had become Raas of his own horde.

"Kaalek," I said, inclining my head to him. "It is good to see you, brother."

His gaze held mine through the screens. "I heard you were in need of assistance."

I bristled at the suggestion that I could not defend my horde, but I did not rise to his bait. If he was not the younger brother who was always trying to best me, I would have welcomed his horde's efforts in the fight. "It is always good to fight alongside my brother." I paused for a beat. "But what are you doing in this sector?"

He clasped his hands behind his back, his tail twitching almost imperceptibly. "I have heard many things of you lately, Kratos. Things that cause me worry."

I fought the urge to laugh out loud. Kaalek had never cared about anything but winning. Even though he was younger than me, he'd always been more eager to accumulate victories and inflict violence.

"I heard you took a human female," he continued, disapproval thick in his voice. "And that the Zagrath have been hunting for her ever since."

"You question my right to take what I want from the enemy?" I growled.

One of his black eyebrows lifted. "You took her from the Zagrath?"

"Not that I owe my younger brother an explanation," I said, leveling my gaze at him. "But she was on a freighter we boarded. It was transporting supplies for the Zagrath."

"And yet you let the ship go." My brother shook his head. "And they have had the enemy after you ever since. I even hear that the sad little freighter searches for you still."

"It is nothing I cannot handle."

"Why not give up your plaything, Kratos?" My brother grinned. "Or are human females really worth all this trouble?"

I strode forward, tearing off my single steel shoulder guard so he could have a better view. "We share mating marks. I will not give her up. It is done."

There was a sharp intake of breath behind me that I knew came from Corvak.

My brother's gaze dropped to the lines that now curled up the side of my neck and down my shoulders. His mouth gaped in genuine shock. Some emotion I'd never seen from him flickered behind his eyes, but was gone a moment later. His voice was a dark purr when next he spoke. "So, they are worth it."

"*She* is worth it," I said.

"I congratulate you, brother." He inclined his head at me. "I only hope this female does not make you soft."

I rested my hand on the hilt of my blade. "Have you ever known me to be soft?"

He grinned at me. "Now that we've eliminated the Zagrath battleship for you, my horde will be returning to our sector. There are a few enemy sympathizers I have my eye on."

"May your raiding be plentiful."

He nodded at me. "And yours."

When he vanished from the screen, Bron let out a loud breath. "What was that about?"

I narrowed my eyes at the screen my brother had filled. "I'm not sure, but when has Kaalek *not* caused trouble?"

CHAPTER
FORTY-ONE

Astrid

I sank up to my chin in the steaming water and let out a moan. Krin had left a little while ago—after I'd noticed that the boy could barely keep his eyes open—and I'd decided to soak away the stress of the day by slipping into the bathing pools in the Raas' suite. I didn't even bother with the cooler water, plunging right away into the crimson pool. Even though I hadn't been involved in any of the battles firsthand, I still felt grimy, and I was certain that my hair held the lingering scent of smoke.

I folded my arms on the dark-stone ledge and rested my head on top of them, letting it loll to one side as the hot water unknotted my muscles. They could say what they wanted about the Vandar being brutes, but there was nothing barbaric about their ships or their technology. Or their baths.

When the water sloshed over the side, my eyes flew open. Before I could turn around, Kratos's large body was cocooning mine as he sank down into the water behind me.

"You're back," I said, my heart still racing. For a huge guy, he could be stealthy when he wanted to be. "Is everything okay?"

"The Zagrath battleship is destroyed and their fleet in shambles. We have won."

I was a little surprised they'd taken out the entire battleship, but I was glad they'd landed a blow against the empire. After spending some time on a Zagrath ship, I understood even more why the Vandar despised them so much. Despite their appearance of being civilized, they were more callous than any raider. "I'm glad. I don't ever want to set foot on one of their ships for as long as I live."

He nuzzled my neck, pressing closer to me, the rigid bar of his cock bumping at the cleft between my ass cheeks. "You won't, and the empire will never take you from me again."

"Because of the mating marks?" I asked, almost hesitant to talk about them with him.

"You were mine before the marks, but now everyone can see the proof of my claim." His arms wrapped around me and his hands touched the black swirls. "Do they hurt?"

I shook my head. "No, and my skin isn't burning anymore."

"That's because we're together." He moved his hands so that they cupped my breasts, and he rolled my nipples between his fingers. "My markings were also hot when we were apart."

Even though his caresses made my legs weak and a rush of heat pulse between my legs, I twisted my head so I could meet his eyes. "So, my skin will burn anytime we're separated?"

"I don't think so. Not since our marks are complete." He nipped at my neck, and a jolt of pleasure skated down my spine. "Now that you are marked as mine."

I let my eyelids flutter closed and dropped my head back to rest on his shoulder. "I'm glad I'm yours."

"Truly?" His voice was husky. "Not because you were forced?"

"You never forced me to do anything I didn't want to," I said, as something soft stroked between my legs—the furry tip of his tail. "I always wanted you way more than I let on."

"Good." His tail parted my legs, then he slipped it between my folds. "I only want to give you what you want, Raisa."

I arched back into him as the tip of his tail circled my clit, a laugh escaping my lips even as my body hummed with desire. "That name actually fits now, doesn't it? I can actually be your Raisa."

"You *are* my Raisa." His voice was darkly dominant, his tail working me in the steamy water and his cock teasing my opening from behind.

"And you are my Raas." I reached back and hooked one hand around his neck, letting my legs lift off the bottom of the pool, while his tail continued to move as expertly as any finger.

My breathing was rapid, and I moved my hips to match his deft strokes, my release building.

"Let go, Raisa," he whispered into my ear. "I want to feel you shatter in my arms."

"Your tail is so good," I said.

"I'm glad you think so," he murmured. "Because I'm about to fuck you with it."

His words made me shake and moan. I dug my fingers into the flesh of his neck as I bucked against him, the waves of my release crashing over me one after the other, leaving me breathless and panting as his tail slid down from my clit and pushed inside me.

It wasn't as thick as his cock, but the tip was hard and the fur thick. Was I actually being tail-fucked by a Vandar warlord? More waves of pleasure crashed over me as he stroked his tail in and out.

"You like my tail in your cunt?" His voice was a purr against my ear.

"Yes, Raas" I managed to say between gasps. "I love anything of yours in my cunt."

"That sounds so good coming from your sweet lips." With a rough growl, Kratos bent me forward, putting my hands on the stone ledge. He pulled his tail out and dragged the crown of his cock through my folds.

"Greedy, Raisa." He pushed his crown inside me slowly. "First I filled you with my tail. Now I'll fill you with my cock."

"Yes, Raas. I want to take all of you."

He gripped my hips and drove his cock deep, making me gasp. "You're sure you can take me? You're so tight."

As my body stretched to take all of him, I made hungry noises. "Your cock is the best kind of hurt, Raas."

He ran a hand up my body, his fingers moving eagerly across the swell of my stomach and the tight peaks of my breasts, feathering over my throat and tangling in my hair. "Tell me you belong to me."

"You know I do," I said as he moved in and out of me with long, hard strokes.

"You are glad that I took you off that ship?"

I moaned. "My life wasn't really worth living before you made that deal with me."

He dragged his cock out, hovering at my opening. "Making that deal was the best decision I've ever made."

"What about the second deal?" I teased.

"You mean my promise that I wouldn't fuck you until you begged me?" He thrust his cock inside me. "That was a mistake. Your little body drove me to the brink of madness before you finally let me claim you."

"I was always yours," I said, my legs trembling. "Even when I was fighting it."

It wasn't just the marks on my body that told me I was the raider's mate. It was the feeling of belonging I felt when I was with him—the knowledge that he saw me, not as I'd always seen myself but as what I *could* be. Raas Kratos had seen the strength that was buried deep within me and had unearthed it, listening to my counsel and making me feel valued. Knowing that I could advise the Raas meant that I was an important part of his crew. *That* made me his, body and soul.

"And I am yours, Raisa," he said through gritted teeth as he stroked deep. "My body, my soul, my cock," he dropped his voice to a dark whisper, "and my tail."

With that, he curled it up between my legs and fluttered it over my clit. I threw my head back, groaning with each deep thrust as my release built again. As my body clenched around his cock and he roared, pounding into me with furious abandon, I knew there was no mate I'd rather have, and nothing I'd rather be than his Raisa.

EPILOGUE

Kaalek

I stomped across the length of my command deck, whirling on one of my warriors. "How can one freighter elude us for this long?"

"It is one freighter, Raas. And this is a large sector."

I grunted, knowing he was right, and I was being unreasonable. Not that a Raas was required to be reasonable. My crew was used to me plunging them into battles that seemed unwinnable and raiding ships that appeared to be too heavily defended. We were always victorious, and we would be this time, as well.

My brother, Raas Kratos, might be fine with letting a ship get away with betraying a Vandar warbird to the Zagrath, but I was not. A strike against any horde was a strike against the entire Vandar people, and I refused to let it be said that the Vandar were merciful.

I had built a name for myself by being more brutal and more terrifying than any other Raas. My elder brother might have more victories—for now—but no raider struck terror into hearts like Raas Kaalek. And now that my brother had taken a human female as a mate, he was bound to turn soft.

My upper lip curled at the thought of a female holding sway over a Vandar warrior. Such a thing would never happen to me. I had no intention of taking a mate until I was too old to serve as Raas. Maybe not even then.

Not that I didn't enjoy the pleasures of a female. I did. It was why my horde frequented the pleasure planet of Lissa so often one of the madams had joked that we were going to establish a colony. But females were fleeting pleasure. I fucked them hard and forgot about them.

Spinning on my heel, I glared at the view of space. Empty space. I opened and closed my fists, aching to swing my battle axe and dish out the punishment that the crew of the Zagrath freighter so dearly deserved.

"Raas." One of my warriors called out, his voice tinged with excitement. "It's the freighter."

"On screen," I ordered, my heart pounding as the image of a battered ship replaced the wide view of space.

"That?" another warrior asked. "We won't even have to use a torpedo to blow that sad ship out of the sky."

I gave a hard shake of my head. "That is too easy for them. We are raiders, are we not?"

"We are boarding the ship?"

I turned to face my warriors. "This scum was shown mercy by my brother and how did they repay that mercy? By sending the empire after him. I intend to show these Zagrath collaborators what happens when you side with the empire."

There was a roar of approval and fists jammed into the air.

"I will lead the boarding party myself." I strode toward the exit of the command deck. "I want to see their eyes when they learn what Vandar justice tastes like."

～

THANK YOU FOR READING POSSESSED!

If you liked this alien barbarian romance, you'll love PLUNDERED, book 2 in the series.

My sister gave herself to the raider warlord to save me. Now I'm hunting him down and getting her back. Even being taken captive by another Vandar warlord won't stop me. I'm immune to his dominant charms—I hope!

One-click PLUNDERED Now>

～

FREE BONUS STORY!! *Want to get a steamy, bonus prequel story about Astrid and Tara before the Vandar arrive? Join my VIP Reader group and get the short story PRELUDE TO POSSESSED!*

https://BookHip.com/SLSCQRD

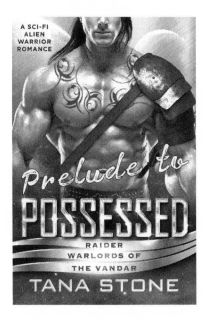

This book has been edited and proofed, but typos are like little gremlins that like to sneak in when we're not looking. If you spot a typo, please report it to: tana@tanastone.com
Thank you!!

SNEAK PEEK OF PLUNDERED—BOOK #2 OF THE RAIDER WARLORDS OF THE VANDAR

Tara

I slammed my palm against the wet tile as the water trickled to a slow drip overhead. "Who do I have to screw to get a decent shower?"

As soon as the words were out of my mouth and echoing back to me in the cramped communal bathroom, I regretted them. I'd done things for much less, and I didn't want to think of what I'd had to do to keep myself and my sister alive.

Pulling the rough towel off a nearby hook, I wrapped it around my chest and stepped out of the shower stall. Not that it had done any good, I thought, as I glanced at my reflection in the warped, reflective metal bolted to the wall. Astrid was gone. After everything I'd sacrificed to keep her safe, she'd been taken captive by a ruthless warlord of the Vandar raiders.

My stomach still roiled when I thought about the day she'd left with the enormous alien. The day she'd *volunteered* to leave with him. That was what hurt the most. She hadn't been dragged off my ship, kicking and screaming. She'd walked off with her head held high.

I stared at myself in the mirrored steel, untying my hair from its topknot and letting the red curls spill down around my shoulders. Then I met my own gaze, the sea-green of my eyes the same color as my sister's and reminding me of the look she'd had when she'd said goodbye to me. She'd been determined. Determined she was doing the right thing. Determined she was saving me.

I tore my gaze away, leaning both hands against the cold basin. That was not the way it was supposed to happen. *I* was the captain of the ship. *I* was the older sister. *I* was supposed to make the sacrifices and take care of her. Not the other way around.

Since our parents had died when I was fifteen and she was twelve, it had been my job to look out for her. It wasn't that my parents had asked me to do it. Their death had been sudden and not something any of us expected. I knew I had to do it because I was the tough one, and my sister would never be able to survive on her own.

I sighed as I thought about Astrid, refusing to imagine her on the raider ship. She was timid and sensitive, a kid who'd always been more perceptive than practical. She could see into someone's soul, but she didn't have an ounce of good sense in her. Which was why she'd been a crap member of my crew, even though I'd moved her from post to post in an attempt to find something aboard my freighter that she excelled at.

It hadn't mattered to me. As frustrated as I could get with her—she was my kid sister, after all—I would never let her fend for herself. Not when I knew she couldn't.

"Why did they take you?" I whispered. It was a question

I'd asked a thousand times in the weeks since she'd been gone.

I'd been willing to take the punishment for her mistake that had gotten us into trouble with the Vandar raiders in the first place. Even if it had meant dying, I was ready to do it to save my sister and save my ship. But then Astrid had gone and ruined it by begging the warlord not to kill me and to kill her instead.

Even though a part of me had never been prouder of her than I had been at that moment, I'd also been furious. She was not supposed to save me. That was my job, and one I'd done well for most of our lives. But on that horrible day, Astrid had been the one to save my life and save the ship, and she hadn't been seen since.

The ship shuddered, bringing me back to reality and reminding me that I needed to return to my post. It was almost first watch, and I always took first watch. Actually, I took most of the watches, since Astrid had vanished with the Vandar horde. Although my freighter was supposed to be delivering supplies to an outpost for the Zagrath Empire, the cargo had been taken by the raiders, and I had a new mission. I had to find Astrid and get her back—no matter what it cost.

My crew wasn't thrilled with our new mission, but so far, none of them had openly challenged me. I was the captain, after all, and I was still paying them, although our money would run out soon enough if we didn't deliver the new cargo we'd picked up for the empire.

I stepped out of the bathroom, making my way quickly down the corridor to my quarters. Luckily, the hall was empty, and the illumination was low. Most of the crew was either in their racks getting sleep, or on the bridge for the fifth watch.

I entered my quarters, edging around my narrow bed in the tight cabin. I was the only member of the crew with an actual cabin, but it was still like a tin can. The attached bathroom was so cramped that I preferred using the communal one down the hall, even though neither had enough water pressure lately for a decent shower.

"I'll get you fixed up soon," I told the ship as I thumped one hand against the wall. "As soon as we get Astrid back, I'll take you in for a full work-up."

I didn't know how I'd pay for that, of course. Once I paid the crew and got supplies, there was rarely anything left for upgrades, or even repairs beyond basic maintenance. Not that I was complaining. Not every twenty-three-year-old woman had her own ship, and I knew how lucky I was to have her.

Lucky was the right word, since I'd won the old freighter in a card game. I'd learned how to gamble from an old card sharp who liked for me to sit on his lap while he taught me. That had been all he liked and all he required, and I'd been more than happy to sit and smile and soak up his knowledge. Not all males asked for so little in return.

The tricks he taught me were the reason Astrid and I hadn't starved, and the reason my sister had never been forced to do any of the things I'd done. Even now, there were few gamblers in the sector who could match my skill. Plenty tried—the powerful aliens hated the thought of being bested by a human female—but they never won.

I pulled open an inset drawer, digging around for something clean to wear. Since our ship's water pressure wasn't working properly, that meant laundry had also been put on hold. I made a face when I realized I'd worn every item in my drawer several times already and none of them smelled clean. If we didn't find Astrid soon, we'd have to stop just because the crew would smell too ripe.

I found a navy-blue button-down and pair of pants that didn't seem too bad, shaking them both out and laying them across the foot of my bed. Opening another drawer, I let out a relieved breath. At least I still had clean underwear.

Despite the fact that I was the captain of a freighter and a deadly gambler, I had a drawer filled with lacy panties and bras. It was my one indulgence and nod to femininity. I tried not to think of the fact that many of the sets had been gifted to me by males who were grateful for my attentions. I told myself that I was using them more than they were using me, and why shouldn't I get something nice in return?

I found my favorite black bra and panties, rubbing my fingers over the sheer fabric and the delicate lace edging before putting them on. These I had bought for myself, which was probably why they were my favorites.

"Today is the day," I said out loud, even though there was no one to hear me. "Today we find Astrid."

I said these same words to myself every day, but every single day I believed them. I had to. If I thought that I would never find my sister and save her from the violent raiders, I wouldn't be able to live with myself. If I even allowed myself to imagine her on the warlord's ship for a second, fear would claw at my throat. Fear that she was being forced by that huge, tailed Vandar, who'd eyed her like she was a meal.

I shook my head again, banishing those thoughts from my brain. My baby sister was fine, and when I tracked down that horde, I would get her back and make sure nothing bad ever happened to her again. Not that I had any idea how a single junky freighter was supposed to force a Vandar horde to do anything, but I would deal with that problem when I had to.

"Captain!" The voice of my first officer crackled over the rusty comms system that fed into my room.

I pressed a panel by the door. "This is Tara. Go ahead."

Static filled the air before he spoke again. "Captain, you should come to the bridge as soon as possible."

My pulse quickened. "Have you found my sister?"

"Not exactly." More static. "More like a Vandar horde has found us."

Before I could ask him anything, the ship shook violently, sending me sprawling to the floor. *Shit. Were they firing on us?*

As I tried to pull myself up, the ship jerked and knocked me down again, my knees hitting the steel floor hard and sending pain shooting up my legs. My skin went cold as I clutched my knees. I knew what that meant. I'd experienced it before—the day Astrid was taken. I'd prayed I would never experience it again.

The Vandar had locked onto us. We were being boarded.

Keep reading HERE

ALSO BY TANA STONE

Raider Warlords of the Vandar Series:
POSSESSED (also available in AUDIO)
PLUNDERED (also available in AUDIO)
PILLAGED (also available in AUDIO)
PURSUED (also available in AUDIO)
PUNISHED (also available on AUDIO)
PROVOKED (also available in AUDIO)

The Tribute Brides of the Drexian Warriors Series:
TAMED (also available in AUDIO)
SEIZED (also available in AUDIO)
EXPOSED (also available in AUDIO)
RANSOMED (also available in AUDIO)
FORBIDDEN (also available in AUDIO)
BOUND (also available in AUDIO)
JINGLED (A Holiday Novella) (also in AUDIO)
CRAVED (also available in AUDIO)
STOLEN (also available in AUDIO)
SCARRED (also available in AUDIO)

The Barbarians of the Sand Planet Series:
BOUNTY (also available in AUDIO)
CAPTIVE (also available in AUDIO)
TORMENT (also available on AUDIO)

TRIBUTE (also available as AUDIO)

SAVAGE (also available in AUDIO)

CLAIM (also available on AUDIO)

CHERISH: A Holiday Baby Short

PRIZE

Inferno Force of the Drexian Warriors:

IGNITE (also available on AUDIO)

SCORCH (also available on AUDIO)

BURN

BLAZE

FLAME

COMBUST

THE SKY CLAN OF THE TAORI:

SUBMIT

STALK

SEDUCE

SUBDUE

ALIEN ACADEMY SERIES:

ROGUE (also available in AUDIO)

All the TANA STONE books available as audiobooks!

INFERNO FORCE OF THE DREXIAN WARRIORS:

IGNITE on AUDIBLE

SCORCH on AUDIBLE

RAIDER WARLORDS OF THE VANDAR:

POSSESSED on AUDIBLE

PLUNDERED on AUDIBLE

PILLAGED on AUDIBLE

PURSUED on AUDIBLE

PUNISHED on AUDIBLE

PROVOKED on AUDIBLE

Alien Academy Series:

ROGUE on AUDIBLE

BARBARIANS OF THE SAND PLANET

BOUNTY on AUDIBLE

CAPTIVE on AUDIBLE

TORMENT on AUDIBLE

TRIBUTE on AUDIBLE

SAVAGE on AUDIBLE

CLAIM on AUDIBLE

TRIBUTE BRIDES OF THE DREXIAN WARRIORS

TAMED on AUDIBLE

SEIZED on AUDIBLE

EXPOSED on AUDIBLE

RANSOMED on AUDIBLE

FORBIDDEN on AUDIBLE

BOUND on AUDIBLE

JINGLED on AUDIBLE

CRAVED on AUDIBLE

STOLEN on AUDIBLE

SCARRED on AUDIBLE

ABOUT THE AUTHOR

Tana Stone is a bestselling sci-fi romance author who loves sexy aliens and independent heroines. Her favorite super-hero is Thor (with Aquaman a close second because, well, Jason Momoa), her favorite dessert is key lime pie (okay, fine, *all* pie), and she loves Star Wars and Star Trek equally. She still laments the loss of *Firefly*.

She has one husband, two teenagers, and two neurotic cats. She sometimes wishes she could teleport to a holographic space station like the one in her tribute brides series (or maybe vacation at the oasis with the sand planet barbarians). :-)

She loves hearing from readers! Email her any questions or comments at tana@tanastone.com.

Want to hang out with Tana in her private Facebook group? Join on all the fun at: https://www.facebook.com/groups/tanastonestributes/